THE

METAPHYSICAL

UKULELE

THE
METAPHYSICAL
UKULELE

STORIES

Sean Carswell

PUBLISHING

New York, New York

Printed in the United Sates of America.
First Paperback Edition
10 9 8 7 6 5 4 3 2 1

Please direct inquiries to:
Ig Publishing
PO Box 2547
New York, NY 10163
www.igpub.com

The following stories originally appeared in the following
publications:

"Mad Nights of Springtime," *The Rattling Wall* and *California Prose
Directory*
"A Place Called Sickness," *Fourteen Hills*
"The Wide Empty Sky," *Thin Air*
"Big Books and Little Guitars," *Fjords Review*
"The Bottom-Shelf Muse," *VLAK: Contemporary Poetics and the Arts*

Library of Congress Cataloging-in-Publication Data

Names: Carswell, Sean, 1970- author.
Title: The metaphysical ukulele / Sean Carswell.
Description: New York, NY : Ig Publishing, [2016]
Identifiers: LCCN 2016005397 (print) | LCCN 2016014399
(ebook) | ISBN 9781632460264 (paperback) | ISBN
9781632460271 (Ebook) Subjects: LCSH: Authors--Fiction. |
BISAC: FICTION / Short Stories (single author). | FICTION /
Literary. | FICTION / Alternative History. | FICTION/ Satire.
Classification: LCC PS3603.A7764 A6 2016 (print) | LCC
PS3603.A7764 (ebook) |
  DDC 813/.6--dc23
LC record available at http://lccn.loc.gov/2016005397

For my mom, who really did give me a notebook when I was seven years old and said, "If you're bored, write a story."

"the only people for me are the mad ones, the ones who are mad to live, mad to talk, mad to be saved, desirous of everything at the same time, the ones who never yawn or say a commonplace thing, but burn, burn, burn like fabulous yellow roman candles exploding like spiders across the stars." —Jack Kerouac, *On the Road*

"But it was heaven there, with ukuleles for harps."
—Thomas Pynchon, *Bleeding Edge*

Table of Contents

Big Books and Little Guitars

Apparently, Herman Melville was a brilliant ukulelist. His biographers tend to leave this part out of his life. Obsessed with his big books, they forget his little guitar. Or perhaps they just get swept away in Melville's South Sea adventures, dreaming about the days after he deserted the *Acushnet* and wandered into the interior of a Polynesian island, convinced he'd find a tribe of beautiful, sexually available women. Or cannibals. Or both. The biographers romanticize Melville's time among the Tai Pī. They speculate about who the real Fayaway was—the Polynesian girl who offered herself to Melville. His very own gift basket. And think of what a treat she must've been for a twenty-year-old, mostly-heterosexual kid from puritanical New England, who had just spent a year at sea without a woman in sight, whose sex life amounted to trading blow jobs with whalers who had no real way of bathing, or else lubing his rod with blubber and masturbating to a little naked woman carved out of a whale bone. A few months with Fayaway must have been everything to him. Fayaway, who saw sex as natural as a breakfast of breadfruit. Who wouldn't be fascinated by Fayaway? Lonely, bearded men in dusty academic offices are more in love with Fayaway than any other word Melville wrote.

When you consider that Melville was unable to walk during his first few weeks with the Tai Pī, and that he was convinced Fayaway was a cannibal, the romance is even wilder. She straddles his erection on a South Sea summer morning, and he wonders if he'll be the main course that night. Will Fayaway join in the feast? Will she think of him fondly as she chews a slice of his wounded thigh?

Of course you'll forget about the ukulele among a scene like this. But make no mistake. It was there.

The first ukulele in the Tai Pī tribe came from a Portuguese missionary. Melville was never clear about what happened to the missionary. Either the missionary left or the Tai Pī ate him. Either way, his *cavaquinho* had been left behind.

The *cavaquinho* changed over the years. Sun and rain caused the wood to warp and crack. The Tai Pī used it as a model and made their own versions of the tiny guitar. When the original strings snapped, they stretched the intestines of one animal or another to make new strings. Melville wondered about those intestines and where they came from. Was he strumming the stretched, dried, and cut digestive tract of the ill-fated missionary? Was Melville desecrating or honoring the missionary's life by strumming a tune from his guts? Would Melville's own guts be strung out over a miro wood ukulele and used to strum an island tune?

After several weeks, Melville's leg healed and all the sex

with Fayaway wasn't enough to shake his haunting visions of the Tai Pī eating him. He nestled the ukulele that Fayaway had given him as a gift and snuck out of the village. Melville carried the Tai Pī uke with him onto his next whaling ship, the *Lucy Ann*.

Conditions were rough on the *Lucy Ann*. The captain kept a close eye on the available food and refused to feed the whalers with enough of it. He wielded his power like the overseer of a Nike shoe factory, slapping his crew around, keeping them hungry, and remaining ever vigilant for new ways make them miserable. While no one murmured the actual word mutiny, the idea floated around before the mast. Amidst this scene, Melville would break out his ukulele. He played it under the Pacific stars, singing songs of Fayaway and freedom and food so plentiful that no one even thought about eating him. Later, after the mutiny went down and the ship docked in Tahiti and everyone but the captain was arrested, one of the sailors on the *Lucy Ann* claimed that Melville's songs inspired the mutiny. And maybe they did. Melville didn't stick around long enough to testify on his own behalf. He slid out of town and into the Tahitian wilds before the authorities got much out of him. Unfortunately, the ukulele was left on the *Lucy Ann*.

In April of 1843, Melville found himself stranded in Hawaii. At this point, he'd deserted two whaling ships and inspired a mutiny on the third. He had a hard time finding a fourth ship to take him back to Nantucket. He worked for a while as a pinsetter in a bowling alley. In the evenings, he played his new taro patch ukulele in a Honolulu brothel. Somewhere lost to history is the man who rolled ten frames set by Herman Melville and listened to Melville strum a few songs on his uke before this Man Lost to History picked out a hooker and slid into one of the brothel's back rooms. This lost man probably never realized that two-thirds of his night's entertainment was brought to him by a sailor who would go on to be regarded as America's greatest author. All the lost man probably remembered the next day was the hooker.

For my part, I can't help thinking of all the high school boys who wish they'd met Melville the way the Man Lost to History did rather than by wading through the cetalogy sections of *Moby-Dick*.

What most people don't realize is that Melville's ukulele nearly led to the death of *Moby-Dick*. The novel, not the whale. It's a complicated story. The first thing that a twenty-first-century reader has to understand is that, in his day, Melville was a bit of a sex symbol. After he wrote his novel about his time with the Tai Pī, after his buddy Toby Greene returned from sea and swore that Melville was pretty much telling the truth with that novel, mid-nineteenth-century readers couldn't shake the image of the bearded rogue Herman Melville and his nights with Fayaway. In fact, Melville was the first American author to hold this dubious status. He had no way to know how to behave. Perhaps the biggest mistake he made was to hang out with critics. He couldn't know about George Burns's famous statement that critics are like eunuchs at a gang bang. George Burns hadn't even been born yet. So this literary sex symbol made his first mistake by hanging out with the metaphoric eunuchs, Evert Duyckinck and William A. Butler.

Melville's second mistake came when he and Duyckinck crashed Butler's honeymoon.

Butler and his new bride were passing through western Massachusetts by train. Melville and Duyckinck met them at the Pittsfield train station. Before William Butler knew what was happening, Melville had absconded with the new Mrs. Butler. The two fled in Melville's carriage and headed for his ancestral manse, the Melvill house. William Butler was left behind to ride with Duyckinck. What happened between the two critics is also lost to history. By the time the critics arrived at the Melvill house, Herman had his ukulele out. The bearded rogue strummed his own composition, a little song called, "I Am the Man from Nantucket." The new bride was on the verge of a swoon. No historian took note of either Duyckinck or Butler's reactions.

A year later, Duyckinck panned *Moby-Dick* in the New York *Literary World*. Butler's review in the *National Intelligencer* was more than a pan. It was downright vicious. He called Melville disgusting and slammed the novel for its "maudlin and ribald orgies."

Again, I can't help thinking of all the high school kids forced to read *Moby-Dick* who would read this review and scream, "What?! There were orgies in that book?! Where?"

Melville's ukulele played the final chord on his friendship with Nathanial Hawthorne, too. And what exactly was going on between Melville and Hawthorne, with Herman so enamored by Nathanial that he bought land next to Hawthorne's farm and moved the Melville family in? What was the subtext behind all of those long, loving letters that Melville and Hawthorne exchanged? Why were the two men so unhappy in the arms of their wives but so pleased with one another?

Maybe it's just me looking too closely into all of this, but when I read about Ahab telling the cabin boy he'll "suck the philosophy from thee," I can't help recognizing that all of Ahab's philosophy is about spermaceti. I feel like I'm in on the joke. And I know of that fateful night on the Hawthornes' farm when Herman Melville broke out the ukulele and strummed his own composition, "You Give Me That Old Natty Glow." Herman smiled as he sang it. Nathanial tapped his foot. Sophie Hawthorne paid perhaps too much attention to the lyrics. She burned red with rage. When the song was over, she turned to her husband and said, "Natty, what the fuck is going on here?"

And, finally, there are the years of failure. The four decades that passed between the time when *Moby-Dick* was published and when Melville died in obscurity. When his greatest work was panned. When he followed it up with a novel called *Pierre*. Really. *Pierre*. When his flop piled upon flop, his debts grew out of control, and he finally had to take a job at a custom house. When his fiction was ignored, his status as literary sex symbol was exchanged for middle-age, then old age. When his bad back and bad reviews relegated the novelist to writing poetry that no one read, and no one reads today. When his wife had enough of him and moved into another bedroom. When his kids had either preceded him in death or swore lifelong grudges against him. When arthritis finally crippled his writing hand.

The only thing left for the aging, obscure Melville was his ukulele. Even if arthritis had taken away his ability to pick the strings, he could still strum. His left hand was still fine, could still dance from one chord to another like jumping fleas. He would nestle the ukulele under his arm and, like so many Manhattoes, follow the streets waterward until he hit the extreme downtown of the Battery. He'd take a bench along the wharves at the southern tip of Manhattan and strum songs for the water-gazers there. Songs about Fayaway and sailors, men from Nantucket and writers who succeeded where he failed. Songs that drifted into the wind and the waves like the legacy he'd never see.

Far Off on Another Planet

Star Wars II: 1978

Leigh Brackett wandered around the empty screening room. The movie everybody else had seen last year shimmered on the wall behind her. She couldn't watch anymore. She didn't care about the kid whining all his lines through his nose, "Threepio, Threepio, where could he be?" This Skywalker punk was no interplanetary hero, no Erik John Stark. He falls into a trash heap with no better ideas than to cry out for his anorexic dandy of a robot.

And she was supposed to make a second blockbuster out of this?

Brackett left the flickering film and the hollow screening room. It was too lonesome to play down there. She set off up the hallway, looking for that little frog of a man who'd hired her for this job. His eyes twinkled when he told stories of the sequel. Somewhere in that sparkle lay the key to unlocking this new screenplay.

Three doors down from the screening room, Leigh turned into George Lucas's office. It was paneled in Philippine mahogany and contained an expensive leather couch, matching armchairs, filing cabinets, and a desk. Lucas's secretary roosted in Lucas's thick leather office chair, legs kicked up, dirt from the soles of his shoes floating down onto the blotter.

"Where's George?," Brackett asked.

Lucas's secretary popped a pistachio into his mouth and started chewing and talking at the same time. "Gone to the impound lot."

"What got impounded?"

"His car." Munch. Munch. Munch. "I guess the Force wasn't with him today."

"Why didn't he send you to get it? Aren't you his lackey?"

Another pistachio popped into that gaping yawp. "He don't let me drive his Bianchina."

Brackett held the secretary's gaze for a brief moment, then, quick as a jungle cat, swatted his feet off the desk and sent him spinning in the chair. "Bounce, kid," she said. "I got writing to do."

The secretary scampered out of the office. Leigh brushed the dust off the blotter and pulled the typewriter close. She fed a sheet into the roller. Since Ed had passed the year before, putting an end to their thirty years of marriage and the force field that had kept illness out of her body, the only thing she could do was write. Writing chased the cancer through her bloodstream, kept the cells that hadn't mutated in fighting shape. The sickness would win. Sooner rather than later. Until it did, she wrote TV pilots that wouldn't be produced and pulp science fiction devoid of Big Thinks. And now this: the sequel to the biggest movie running.

Before typing, she dug into Lucas's bottom drawer in hopes of finding a bottle there. Howard Hawks always had a bottle. Writing went smoother with it around. And, let's face it, with Howard around. This Lucas kid was different. Where she expected to find a bottle she found a ukulele. "This, that, or the other," she said to herself, lifting the uke from the drawer. "As long as it loosens the fingers."

Lucas's ukulele had an internal cold to it that Brackett couldn't make sense of. It was like the uke had been stored in a faraway ice planet where night brings death and rebels bunker against impending doom. The sound was off, too. These Big Fellas with their Big Ideas and their tin ears. Brackett hummed an A and tightened the top string into tune. From there, it was short work to get the other strings to sound right.

Cold or not, the ukulele felt good in Leigh's hands. It had one of those strong, vibrant necks that was pleasant to graze her thumb against. Brackett plucked a few notes and let the cold and sounds take her to that icy world.

The Big Sleep: 1945

From the beginning, when Hollywood needed someone to write like a man, Brackett was the woman they called. It started with Howard Hawks when the Big War was still running. He had ol' Bill Faulkner scribbling away on a script for *The Big Sleep*, and all Bill could do was talk about the stains of sin and the crimes of history. So Howard phoned Leigh's agent, balked when he found that Leigh was a woman's name, but sent for her anyway.

She showed up with her brown curls bouncing under a beret. So young then. She looked nice. She looked very nice indeed. The soft wool of her dress was gathered and bloused, so that her full sharp curves were hinted at rather than seen, and the way the whole thing was cut made her look taller and slimmer. Howard took one glance and said, "Jesus, what are you? I was expecting a truck driver of a broad. You look like a God damn Howard Chandler Christie painting."

Maybe Brackett was a tangle of nerves inside, but she'd be damned if that came out. "Mister," she said, eyes locked on Hawks'. "We both know you didn't hire me to play tennis."

Howard smiled. "Well, at least you can spar." He ushered her down to Faulkner's bungalow. Bill was a contract writer. A 9:30 to 5:30 guy. The most important writing he did every day was his name on the time card coming and going.

Howard barged in without knocking. Bill's secretary, a wavy-haired beauty in wide-legged trousers and monochrome flats, popped out of her chair. Loose papers scattered about her feet. She held out her hand to greet Howard and Leigh. The ink stain on her right middle finger glistened in the Hollywood light pouring in from the doorway.

"Meta Carpenter," Howard said, with a nod to the secretary. "Used to work for me. Now I can't pull her out of Bill's bungalow."

Leigh shook Meta's ink-stained hand.

Meta said, "Charmed."

Bill remained seated on a Baltimore fancy side chair. He wore a tweed coat pockmarked with cigarette burns, ashy slacks, and a bow tie tilted to tickle the left side of his chin waddle. He played something intricate on a banjolele. It sounded gothic and classical, but also somehow contemporary and new. Leigh felt yanked out of her body and into the universe of Faulkner's song. It was all off. She'd built enough worlds to know. The composition may be brilliant, but the tempo wavered out of time signatures and the floating bridge had floated upwards, sabotaging the little instrument's intonation.

Meta rescued Leigh from her trance. "The little banjo is on loan from Ray Chandler."

"It's lovely," Brackett said, less about the instrument than about the way the secretary's aristocratic twang breezed into the song.

Hawks had no time for any of this. He snapped, "Bill!"

Faulkner struggled to lift his gaze from the weight of his heavy eyelids. He seemed to live behind a wall eight feet thick. "Howard," he said, slow and soft, as if the name had too few syllables so he'd necessarily drag each one through its own airburst.

"Put down that God damn little toy and meet your new co-writer, Leigh Brackett."

Leigh stepped forward to greet Faulkner. Bill leaned the banjolele against a tin trash can. He grabbed a copy of Chandler's *The Big Sleep* and flipped to the middle page.

"Should you be agreeable to a simplified collaboration of this endeavor, I propose we divide our labors equally. I'll bay the front half of this bear while you come around and assault from the rear."

Leigh turned to Hawks for a translation. "He'll write the first half; I'll take care of the second?"

Faulkner blocked Hawks' reply by grabbing both halves of the cheap paperback and struggling to tear it down the spine. The glue held strong and the pages, while fluttering like butterflies gathered in a net, refused to rip. Faulkner grunted and pulled, but proved no match for the pulp. Leigh wondered if everyone was embarrassed, or just her.

Howard barked, "Enough of this nonsense. Meta, tell Leigh what she'll write. Let's get this show on the road."

It took eight days to write the script. Bill went on a bender for three of them. Meta signed his time cards for him. Leigh worked in the adjacent bungalow, on contract from Howard and not from the studio. As long as pages were typed, Howard didn't bother with hours. Late mornings and long lunches flew just fine. Leigh's only restriction was the ten o'clock curfew her mother insisted on. Brackett could've written it all at home, and faster, but for her aunt constantly interrupting, asking time and again why Leigh didn't write something nice, something *Ladies Home Journal* would buy. It was worse than the screams from Bill and Meta in the bungalow next door. At least Meta could stand on her own, give Bill as bad as she got, happy to scream, "Your wife," whenever something needed breaking.

On the eighth day, Bill stopped by Brackett's bungalow for tea. Meta stayed behind to type up pages from an opening scene between Philip Marlowe and General Sternwood. Faulkner brought his banjolele along. Leigh took it from him with all the gentleness of an Army doctor extracting a Mauser slug from a GI's thigh. She strummed a tune, simple and sweet and with enough empty spaces between notes for her to slide the floating bridge into place and tighten the slack skin. When the sound was right, she handed it back to Bill, knowing his ear would never know the difference.

Star Wars II: 1978

Lucas peered up at the screen. The light from a gunfight in an intergalactic saloon splattered across his face. Something about his fascination with his own film was totally inhuman. His bright, intent eyes showed a curious mixture of intelligence and what could be madness.

Leigh sat next to him and finger-picked the icy ukulele. She played along to the score of the film. This was her favorite part. The intergalactic saloon band knew only one song. The repetition of it left light years of space for her to improvise in. Brackett had sat in this screening room with this film so many times that the score had taken residence inside the twisted channels of her ear. Her ukulele improvisations had become the newest and freshest part of the film.

And here it was, Leigh would think when she wasn't thinking about the sequel. Here was her art in a nutshell.

The form was rigid, intractable, beyond her control. But what she could do in those tiny pockets of silence between notes, it was Big. Even if only she heard it.

George would tap his foot along with her ukulele. He'd never address it directly. She'd doctored enough scripts, done enough contract writing to know how to be invisible, how to contribute things that seemed to grow in place rather than be created by someone else. So when George heard the ukulele, Leigh was sure he heard it as something that he'd thought of first, that had been there all along.

And George was a sweet kid. At the beginning of the movie, when the whiny hero was still in his desert home, George had asked, "Recognize this place?"

"Sure," Leigh said. She'd been to Arizona, driven over from Lancaster. Her and Ed passed through this very patch of dunes on the way to Tucson for one of those Hawks movies. *Rio Bravo* maybe. Or, no. *El Dorado*.

"It's your Mars," George said. "Exactly how I pictured it when I read your stuff in *Planet Stories* as a kid."

George's hand gripped tightly around the arm of the theater chair. Leigh patted his wrist, felt the tendons tighten under her fingers. "It's perfect," she said.

But it was not perfect. None of it was perfect. She could feel the sickness thicker in her blood with every day in the screening room. Most times, when the ukulele got too cold and the film seemed to stretch across eons, she could up and leave. Get back to writing, which was what she was being paid to do, anyway. Lucas kept insisting she watch the movie. She couldn't make it through. Even with George right next to her in this cozy screening room.

Silent as cats except for the gentle rattle and whisper of tiny pills in a plastic bottle, Leigh took some of the medicine the doctor prescribed to her. The pills wouldn't cure anything. They wouldn't even take away the pain. They would just make her feel a little better about the final scenes in life she had left. Leigh swallowed a small handful with a gulp of water. It settled into her stomach like the distillate of all the sweet wickedness of the world.

George was now perched at the front of his seat, his arms wrapped around the seatback in front of him, his knees nearly touching the carpeted floor. As flashes of a laser battle flickered across his face, she pictured him as an ancient, a trainer of old screenwriters and young Jedi knights alike. She'd call him Minch. Luke could carry all of her frustrations with Minch's Force. Artoo could be her cancer, beeping and whirring as a constant reminder that he wasn't happy with any of this.

From another room, Lucas's secretary called the boss away. George, legs asleep, wobbled out of the screening room.

Brackett settled back into her chair. Her last thought before drifting off to sleep was her first rule of writing: the guy who signs the final check has the final say.

El Dorado: 1965
Howard and Leigh were back in Tucson. The wintertime desert felt worlds away from the Ohio ranch where Leigh

and Ed did their writing in adjoining studies, Mars to the Venus of her marital home. The distance apart was mitigated by the script she'd written for El Dorado. It was her finest work yet. It wasn't tragic, but it was one of those things where John Wayne dies at the end. Hawks said he loved it. The studio loved it. Wayne loved it. "All it needs," Howard said, "is a little polish on it."

He flew Leigh and Ed out to Los Angeles for this polish. Ed took up residency in their home in Lancaster. Leigh followed Howard from LA to southern Utah to Tucson. "A little polish on it," Leigh knew, could mean anything from rewriting damn near the whole thing to just rewording dialogue enough to make a man out of a Mitchum or Wayne. She brought along her traveling typewriter. Lightweight, speedy keys, always at the ready.

Good thing, too, because "a little polish on it" this time meant taking the finest thing she'd written and turning it into a remake of *Rio Bravo*, which she'd written already.

The waning sun streaked the mesas a blood orange on the outskirts of Tucson. Gaffers and grips rolled cords and folded screens. Camera men packed their lenses and stored the dailies. Robert Mitchum headed off for the nearest bar, looking like nothing more than a tin badge pinned to a drunk. John Wayne loitered around the director and the writer, waiting to petition for an extra line or an extra one after that. Howard said, "I need some new lines."

Leigh felt it coming like a sap to the back of the neck. "I wrote you new lines," she said. "What you want is some old ones."

Howard swatted Leigh's words away like so much desert dust gathered into the fibers of his slacks. "It's where the girl comes into town..."

"Which girl?" Leigh asked. "Angie Dickinson?"

"Sure. Angie. Whatever the hell her name is," Howard said.

Duke interjected. "Angie's not in this movie. The girl has to be Charlene or Michele."

"Charlene. Michele. Angie. What's the difference? The girl comes in on a stage and blah blah blah. You get it Leigh?"

"I get it." The desert seemed to have drifted into Brackett's mouth. Grains of sand ground into her back molars. "I wrote the damn scene eight years ago."

Duke looked down at Leigh from a perch that felt about eight feet above her. "That's right," he said. "If it was good once, it'll be just as good again."

Leigh stomped off to her trailer, lines for Angie or Charlene or Michele racing through her head. She typed with a view of the sunset spectacular out her window. She wrote until the dark shut down.

Star Wars II: 1978

Leigh dropped off the first draft of the sequel with Lucas. George wore no mask between himself and his excitement. If he'd had a tail, he would've wagged it. "I can't wait," he said, short of breath like even the words took him away from the reading he wanted to do. "I'm going to read this right now." His eyes didn't rise from the page to address Brack-ett. She watched his glance dart across the words. This must have been what a young George looked like when his new issue of *Super Science Stories* arrived in his Modesto mailbox, when he raced inside and tucked himself into his father's oversized armchair and read "The Citadel of Lost Ships." Leigh gave herself a few moments to indulge in this fantasy, to think of all the boys and men so excited to swallow the pulp that she and Ed had been grinding out for most of the middle of this century. When the moments passed, she remembered the most important thing.

"Um, George, honey," she said. "There is the matter of my check."

Brackett's words ripped Lucas from his ice planet and back to this dark mahogany office. He gulped air against the bends. "Yes. Yes," he said. "Of course." He reached into the bottom drawer of his desk, extracting his ukulele. A pay-check was woven into the strings. "I know you played it to help yourself write," he said. "Take it. Take it and the money. It was always too cold for me, anyway."

Leigh stuffed the check into her purse. The check itself was the size of all checks. The number on it was large enough to take care of her for the rest of her life, a span of time she knew couldn't be more than a few weeks. She cradled the ukulele in her arms. It was preternaturally cold as it had always been. George's mind jumped into hyperspace. He landed on the ice planet before Leigh could say goodbye.

She headed down the hallway. Lights had been extinguished. Night awaited outside.

Leigh knew she'd written her final work. It was better than the *Star Wars* that had come before it. Brackett—whose heroines had never simpered or fainted, melted or whimpered—had taken a lot of the princess out of Leia. She'd given the character some of the old verve Brackett had given Bacall back in the war years. Maybe that dancer's daughter could do something with those lines. She'd given Han Solo a father who could teach him how to be a man. She made Luke, the whiny little blond kid, into a real hero, one who could best Darth Vader in hand-to-hand combat at the end. And the scenes with Minch were the best. Leigh was certain George would love them.

Of course, she also knew that some younger version of a Brackett would come along and put a polish on her screenplay. There was no telling how much of a polish, what would get shined up and what would get shined off. She only knew polishing would occur.

Brackett held the cold ukulele close to her breast, chilling the metastasized blood inside. "I'll be there soon, Ed," she said, pushing the studio door open.

She stepped into the starlight.

Mad Nights of Springtime

In the lettuce fields of postwar America with a cold Pacific fog drifting over the Santa Clara River valley just north of Los Angeles, a young Jack Kerouac wandered into the campsite of itinerant Filipino farmhands. He was not even thirty; not yet on the verge of a fame that would come to destroy him. The farmhands strummed their Catholic hymns on a ukulele. Little Jack, Ti Jean as his blesséd old French Canadian mother called him, felt the air vibrated by song and strings and experienced the satori to carry him into the great nothing. It was beginning and end.

As with any great religious observance, the farmhands kept wine nearby. An old, thin man waved Jack in. The old man's giant hands were all out of proportion for the bony arms they dangled at the end of. Those hands—too big for picking strawberries or blueberries or any berries but just the right size to cradle a cabbage in his palm—welcomed Jack and pointed to a seat where Jack sat and accepted the circling bottle of wine and sang along. Could they be singing in English? Yes, Jack. It's "I'll Take You Home Again, Kathleen" with thick pidgin accent. This song so much like the songs of Lowell in that tender childhood, father still alive, brother still alive, everyone alive and in love with this beautiful world that postwar America could now only see as prewar America. Prewar America couldn't have known they were pre-anything. Nor could the young rootless Jack, wandering on the road that would become On the Road, know he was pre-Kerouac.

So Jack sang along. A farmhand straight out of Hawaii like so many of these farmhands who left the sugar plantations of the Big Five or the pineapple fields with its barbs tearing through every glove and cloth to hunch down in the foggy soil of row crops passed the ukulele along to Ti Jean. The sweet little nun who had soothed Jack's hands, knuckles bruised from her sisters in the cloisters, by teaching him to play the guitar in those long gone beautiful days of Lowell and now he knew how to hold those slender fingers, so dexterous from days at the portable typewriter, into chords at least guitar chords and those ears so good for dialog could also hear the difference between an A and a G and could find the notes of a scale. Pretty soon the Filipino farmhands taught Jack to play the song that the Mexican farmhands had taught them, a simple three-chord arrangement that invited all to dance not like a sailor but like the captain. Jack played the song. Families of farmhands clapped and sang along and banged blesséd camp spoons against camp cooking tins and swung babes in arms and held sweethearts close in order to dance (*para bailar la bamba*).

As the wine dwindled down and sweethearts and mothers and fathers with babe in arms lay down to rest for the night and even the thin old man with his giant hands could wrestle only scattered seconds of awakened consciousness between deep snoring rhythms, Jack searched the strings and notes of that old taro patch instrument until he found the chords for "Is You Is or Is You Ain't My Baby?" He sang it softly to the valley and fields and Filipino farmhands and his lovely Mexican girlfriend in the adjacent camp with her crazy brothers mumbling "*mañana*" in their sleep. This America.

In the mad nights of springtime Corte Madera many years later, Locke McCorkle gifted Jack a handmade ukulele. Locke made the uke himself, carved the neck from a trunk of sun-hardened myrtle felled right on the property where Locke built his home and the guest shack where Jack and Gary Snyder lived that spring. The back and sides were made of that same myrtle milled down to thin planks matched with a thin piece of ancient redwood for a soundboard. One strum and the air vibrated with the natural sounds of Bay Area, 1956. Jack quickly learned to play folk songs to be sung by the fire and songs *para bailar*. He played these on nights and parties in McCorkle's house, Locke and wife nude and dancing with Gary nude with nude girlfriend and nude Allen Ginsberg and nude Peter Orlovsky and even clothed Philip Whalen on the side tapping a nude foot and Jack the itinerant *bhikkhu* sadly strumming upbeat songs. He developed a way of playing the uke spontaneously. The first note was always the best note. Songs followed a loose pattern of solitary introspection and solitary introspection with mad wild parties in between. All songs sounded similar but each was its own unique experience. Improvisation never to be repeated. Nude Locke and nude Gary and nude Allen and nude Peter and nude women and *bodhisattvas* all demanded songs they could dance to. Jack's spontaneous sounds were abandoned during the parties. Structured strumming of pop songs took their place. Later, though, sitting atop his little feather sleeping bag in deep grass next to Gary's little cabin in the hills with Gary asleep or off with one of his many women, Jack played his deepest painful pleasure in solitary celebration. First note, best note. Always.

Locke's wife sewed a padded bag for the ukulele, specifically designed to cradle the soft redwood soundboard and hold the uke close to Jack's revolutionary rucksack. With rucksack on back and Locke already at work for the day and Locke's wife and children cleaning away to the sounds of the living room hi-fi, Charlie Parker spinning at 78 rpm, Jack knelt in honor of the Corte Madera innocence that would soon be lost (could he know this at the time?) in a summer of desolation and an autumn of scandal and explosion.

On Desolation Peak, Ti Jean barely touched his ukulele. He stared at the redwood grains and dreamed of Corte Madera and the parties and the friends and the social life that on the peak had been reduced to nightly radio conversations discussing muffin recipes. Jack traced the flaming patterns of myrtle waving along the neck. He picked up the ukulele and dreamed of times playing with farmhands and beatniks, or of playing guitar with nuns or toying with a *cuatro* for the lovely Esperenza Villanueva. The first note was no better than any other note because no Desolation Peak note was played into the silence that surrounds us all for eternity.

On the way down the mountain, Jack found the *dharma* in charity by giving his ukulele to a wild, beatific Oregon wrestler with shoulders so much like Gary's sculpted out of logging and trail adventures in the rainforest west of the Cascades. The wrestler drove Jack as far south as Grants Pass. Jack said goodbye to both wrestler and ukulele with a "Blah" that he understood to say it all.

Back in San Francisco, without the spontaneous uke to keep him rooted, Jack fell into wine and howling poets. His old pal Greg Corso had migrated west to join the madness. Corso spent most days chafing the patience of Allen and Peter and especially Kenneth Rexroth for whom Kerouac was all too happy to chafe. Neal Cassady had moved back in with wife Carolyn and two kids, back to working for the railroad and embracing the work/produce/consume ideology of Ike Eisenhower and William Levitt and even aspiring to shortcut his way in like a Midnight Ghost funded on winnings at the horse track. Allen's "Howl" was finally being heard and not only heard but (could they know then?) hunted down by Captain Hanrahan of the San Francisco PD in hopes of saving the children of SF from the greatest minds of a generation who blew and were blown by ecstatic bikers. The machinery was too much for Jack.

When Locke finally met a woebegone Jack on the North Shore, Locke seeking a pre-workday meal and Jack ending a wild night in search of eggs enough to soak up a belly full of Tokay, Jack nearly burst into tears (Catholic guilt). Locke took Jack to a nearby diner and purchased two plates of ham and eggs. Locke shoveled eggs potatoes ham into his hungry mouth. Jack used fork to push his eggs around the porcelain, crashing from ham to hash brown. Locke wouldn't speak of the ukulele. Truth be told he was disappointed. Sure the ukulele was Jack's to keep or give away as he saw fit but really for the forty hours Locke spent milling and carving and sanding and gluing and rubbing oil into the wood and the twenty-seven hours Locke's wife spent cutting and padding and sewing the case, the ukulele was Jack's to keep only. Locke held his disappointment inside and smiled his beatific Buddha grin and said, "You have no idea how good these hams and eggs is. If you had any idea whatsoever how good these hams and eggs is, you'd quit your sulking and dig in."

Jack mumbled, "These hams and these eggs, them hams and them them eggs."

It was the eternal suppertime in Park Avenue penthouse apartments. With *On the Road* a bestseller and *Subterraneans* and *Dharma Bums* hot on its heels and every TV talk show host hungry to drag a drunken Jean-Louis Kerouac in front

of a camera as a spark to the Society of the Spectacle, Ti Jean
wore his forty-dollar sport coat and headed into Manhattan
to dine with Steve Allen. Steve played his piano like an old
American patriarch in his Upper East Side loft apartment
with direct elevator access while his wife Jayne cooked dinner. Jack refused to read poems to Steve's accompaniment,
though they'd recorded together and performed live on television together already. Jack had time to feel ashamed and
to feel the pain of his failed rucksack revolution straying far
from its prophecy. Instead, he had drifted in front of the
eyes of thousands of Americans staring at the same thing
and on some nights that same thing was him and not his
thoughts or his poetry but his drunken disheveled look in
his forty-dollar sport coat clashing with barbershop haircut
and slacks bought three-for-a-dollar at the local Goodwill.
Jack relented not to perform his poetry but to play Steve's
ukulele. It was not a taro-patch, straight from Hawaii and
played in the fields to songs sung in pidgin accents nor the
holy ancient redwood myrtle handmade by ancient *bhik-
khus* but a mass-produced, Arthur Godfrey model ukulele
made in Chicago for people to purchase and never play after
watching Godfrey's music hour. They ate fine pork chops
with green bean accompaniment. They played songs and
told stories. Steve offered Jack a bottle of brandy as sacra-
ment. After many glasses, Jack got drink drunk he got. He
came to like old Steve a little better. Holy Steve, forever
flawed, forever seeking enlightenment. For Steve alone Jack
twisted his face and pointed finger to the sky in honor of the

bodhisattva comedian Dayton Allen and recited the mantra, "Whyyyyyy **not**?"

Jayne asked Jack about recording with jazz saxophonists Zoot Sims and Al Cohn and Jack told her of carrying his great holy suitcase full of handwritten haikus to the recording studio where Zoot tooted and Cohn blown and that bebop tick tock jazz filtered through. Only Zoot and Al didn't stick around for the playback and Ti Jean huddled in a corner and cried. When he retold the story, he left out the crying. He held his Arthur Godfrey ukulele close and plucked a perfect note to salve the seething wound that the brandy could no longer sooth. That moment coincided with holy American patriarch Steve Allen and his long-suffering Jayne thanking Jack for a wonderful night as a way of saying, "Jack, it's time to go now." But Jack undaunted borrowed black telephone and rang an army of beatniks to roam Manhattan streets forever in a southerly direction.

Three years Jack spent holed up with his mother on Long Island and fame surrounding him and television appearances and penthouse patriarchs and beatniks hanging on to a phony lifestyle that was honest in books but lost in translation to action when actions became repetitions instead of spontaneous. Finally, he heard that engine calling all cars back to the end of the land sadness, end of the earth gladness. He used his mother's phone to ring Lawrence Ferlinghetti over at the now-canonized City Lights Bookstore where they hatched a plan for Ti Jean's surreptitious slide through San Francisco and down to Big Sur where the real writing, the poetry of "Sea," could commence. He was to arrive by cross country train with a ticket this time, indoors with no flapping arms or beatific bums saying prayers to Saint Theresa, and call the saintly City Lights using an alias. Lawrence would shuttle Jack disguised in fishing hat and slickers down to the cabin near Bixby Bridge where they would dine with Henry Miller. No wine but intoxicating conversation. Only Jack didn't call first but stumbled into City Lights where the fishing hat and slicker proved no disguise and a three-day bender commenced. First drunk, best drunk.

One fast move took him by bus to Monterey and cab to Bixby Creek where he passed out in a field with an ornery old mule licking his face. Henry Miller had given up on Jack four days earlier. He needed no other introduction. Lawrence Ferlinghetti was done waiting. Saintly City Lights called. He gathered Ti Jean up and took him to the grocery store to amass dry goods and perishables and escorted Jack to the cabin before heading north up the Pacific Coast Highway. Jack was left alone in the cabin. He wandered the fields. He listened to the sea. He practiced haikus written to the ornery mule:

> Pacific patriarch
> reincarnated from Manhattan penthouse
> lick my face—sploosh!

He also found Ferlinghetti's perfect heavenly ukulele carried back from days of a Pacific theater that performed a new tragedy and endowed the survivors with ennui and existential void. For three weeks, Jack played his spontaneous uke. He carried it down Bixby Creek to a cave overlooking the ocean roaring with choruses of waves fifteen feet high. The sea air and hours of spontaneous strumming took its toll. Iodine crept into the glue holding the blesséd ukulele together. It choked Jack's deep breath. He felt his own glue returning to liquid form. One fast move and he was gone.

What remained was not, was never the air Ti Jean vibrated on his own.

The Song at the Bottom of a Rabbit Hole

The Five of Swords continues to haunt Patricia Geary. He shows up daily. She sits at her kitchen table with its view of bougainvillea creeping along a shadowbox fence. Hummingbirds suck from the pink flowers. Pat pushes aside wayward student manuscripts and the crusty oatmeal bowl that her husband neglected to remainder in the sink. She lays down three cards. The Five of Swords emerges as one. He is a warning or a reminder of ego struggles and pyrrhic victories. Every morning.

He's a mysterious character this number Five, standing alone with two swords stacked in his arms and three swords scattered about his feet. Two vanquished fighters wander away.

Of course, Pat knows how to read the card. She knows what it means and how to apply it to her life, but it's the artwork on this particular deck that sends her down a rabbit hole.

The victor who has gathered the swords looks off. Presumably, he'd be a warrior. Who but a warrior would want five swords? But this victor looks more artist than warrior. His shirt is tattered, frayed at the edges, falling apart not with the slashes of enemy swords or the outstretched fabric of a tussle, but threadbare from too many wearings, too many washings. There isn't a bloodstain to be found on the blouse. Even if there were, Pat is certain she'd read it as red acrylic paint. Or maybe catsup.

And the victor's countenance in three-quarter profile, facing the edge of the card while his round, soft eyes glance back at the vanquished: he has the beautiful and innocent façade of a seducer, of a man who tenderly fills his wife's pipe with opium. Pat knows that face. It originally belonged to Dante Gabriel Rossetti.

Regardless what the card means, Rossetti's face is the real ghost, the real haunting.

At moments like this, Pat seeks solace in her ukulele.

Times haven't called for this consolation in so long that she isn't sure exactly where she can find the ukulele. Somewhere in her home office. Somewhere buried deep in the geologic layers, in a strata she dates as 1987. The excavation will take the better part of an afternoon. Just the barrier of dolls, stacked like Day-Glo cannonballs and keeping vigil with their huge eyes, will take a few hours of gentle movement.

With brown paper bags from Trader Joe's substituting for a fossil hammer, Pat begins digging.

Many hours later, around midnight, Pat sits in her office chair and scans the room. Heaped in brown grocery bags are the archives of a writer's life, which, so far, seems to have been dedicated to the accumulation of worldly goods.

Pat knows what the average mystic has to say about worldly goods: clutter is evil; simplicity is good. But somewhere inside her Pat wonders if this dichotomy itself isn't a little too much simplicity.

Regardless, the brown paper bags sit full of snapshots of loved ones, school pennants, stories written by aspiring undergraduates, and a variety of once-meaningful effluvia: a first-place certificate, neatly folded, along with the blue ribbon, for the Vista Junior Talent Contest; a yarn voodoo doll; a turtle-shaped pincushion; a ballerina jewelry box; a Ginny doll missing half a leg; imitations of reproduction Blythe dolls; a toy poodle with its fur darkened from the oil and dirt of a younger Pat's fingers; a mysterious piece of brick with the single letter P; old issues of *Marie Claire* and *Vogue*; entire series of mystery novels dedicated to knitting, antiquing, and psychics; acrylic yarn in colors that went out of style a decade ago; single knitting needles missing their partner. Bag after bag after bag.

Atop the bag nearest her, Pat glimpses again a letter from the Philadelphia Science Fiction Society, the overseers of the Philip K. Dick Award, inviting her to Norwescon in lovely Tacoma, Washington for the award ceremony. Pat and four other finalists would read from their work. One finalist would win. Pat, of course, won. That was a Five of Swords memory.

Unlike most people, Pat was absent when her life changed irrevocably. The gears that would control the machinations of her future turned in Manhattan while Pat vacationed in Lake City, Florida. It was the holiday season, 1986.

Pat took a stroll through the woods near her mother's home. She wore a cape—always a risky fashion choice. The key, Pat knew, was to wear the cape rather than letting the cape wear you. Superheroes: they let the cape wear them. The cape wore Superman so strongly it carried him into the air, forcing him into a perpetual plank pose. Batman tried to use his cape to tuck his love for a Boy Wonder under while Robin's love for Batman was broadcast in the fluttering red cloth flowing behind him. Pat draped her cape over her shoulders, keeping her warm on a cool Florida morning. Confidence was key. Pat pulled it off while roaming across campus in Baton Rouge, but here in Florida, with her sister picking at every random hair on Pat's skin, the cape was a more nebulous proposition.

It followed Pat into the woods.

The conifers of Northern Florida stretched, long and lean, into the gray sky. A young boy scaled the thin trunk of a nearby pine. Pat sat to watch his progress. He shuttled up the tree with a competence familiar to all primates but the human kind. The tree buckled under the boy's weight. It bowed, impossibly, to the ground. For a tense second, Pat watched as the tree formed a pine archway and set the boy down on the carpet of needles at the forest floor. The boy climbed off. The tree whipped back into place.

Snap!

The boy raced off for another tree. Before he would've

had time to climb it, Pat heard another snap. A cursory inspection of the forest unearthed a group of boys, all climbing the thin, flexible pines until the trees touched their tops to the forest floor. Pat settled in for the spectacle.

Through the fog of the waxing day, another figure walked toward Pat. Pat drank him in. Where had he found this gorgeous ensemble? His indigo tuxedo contrasted smartly with a billowing white silk shirt and charcoal brocade jodhpurs. Neat gray suede boots peeked out from beneath the cuffs and long, slender fingers were covered with lambskin gloves.

Pat had never met this gentleman in a nonfictional world, but she knew him.

Sammy.

Sammy sat next to Pat. Pat shivered, though the cool Florida woods were not cold enough to elicit a shiver, though her cape wrapped around to keep her snug. She had the impulse to be nice, to set this conversation on friendly terms despite Sammy's ominous aura. She said, "I like your suit."

The statement dropped like a nickel falling on a hardwood desk, rattling in its understatement.

"There are laws," Sammy said.

Pat felt something like a shot put drop to the bottom of her stomach.

The group of boys continued to climb on and climb off the pines. Snaps echoed throughout the woods. Pine tops wobbled.

"There are laws for everything. Thieving, for instance."

He leaned closer, his ice-chip eyes glittering in the faint traces of morning sun.

"My book." The words came out before Pat considered them. She wasn't sure which book she referred to. A few years earlier, her novel *Living in Ether* had come out. Perhaps she'd leaned a bit too much on the works of Yukio Mishima, but that was an influence, not a theft. And what about *Strange Toys*, sitting on a desk at Bantam in Manhattan. Too much Angela Carter? Too much Lewis Carroll? Could a writer steal one novel from two people?

Who was the real thief here, and what were they stealing?

Sammy said, "Writers steal things. Writers don't know what to do with them."

"Who are you?" Pat asked.

"You know my name," Sammy said. "And I have something you need."

"Me?"

"There is danger ahead for your novel. But there is always a way around every law. Each law with the penalty attached, each system connected to another system. Because you have something I want, I'm prepared to…"

One of the tree-climbers ran toward Pat and Sammy, not as if he were running to them, but as if they didn't exist, and he could run through the space occupied by them. The boy paused and met Pat's glance.

Pat knew what the boy saw, what everyone saw looking into Pat's face: that expression yearning toward some other world. That expression which seemed to piss people off and make them suspicious. The boy was no exception. He snarled at Pat. His twisted lips stretched the freckles on his face. His blond crew-cut glistened with dew slicked onto him from the pines he climbed. At that moment, he looked like every cocky boy who pursued Pat in high school and turned his failure to capture Pat into a hatred for her.

The boy said, "Nice cape, lady."

More than anything, Pat was surprised that Sammy, with his indigo tux and jodhpurs, got a free pass while Pat's cape was the object of backwoods scorn. She turned to see Sammy's reaction, but Sammy was gone.

The boy, too, scurried off for another flexible pine.

Pat gathered herself to return to her mother's. She stood and brushed the needles off her slacks. Tracing the path of a pine needle on its way to the forest floor, Pat saw at her feet a ukulele. The instrument either came from Sammy or came from nowhere. Pat was half-convinced that Sammy had only been metaphysical. Thus, the ukulele would have to be metaphysical.

It sat on the carpet of pine needles, cute as a pug. Even the grains of dark wood reminded Pat of a pug's short hairs.

If the ukulele had had a tail, it would've wagged at Pat.

Pat reached down and rubbed the ukulele's neck. The ukulele jumped into her arms. She stroked the strings and heard the familiar tune: My Dog Has Fleas.

She started walking back to her mother's house, her cape fluttering in the wind and the ukulele trotting along in step with her.

Somehow, she knew her novel was doomed.

The evening after Pat's stroll among the arching pines in the forests of North Florida, Sammy struck. Pat's writing career careened down the one-way path of entropy; she'd no more be able to recreate the past of it than she could turn a sapling back into an acorn or shrapnel back into a grenade.

The moment of the Five of Swords cut in Pat's absence. While she celebrated the growing Christmas season in Florida, her editor accepted that one drink too many at a holiday party in the Bantam offices.

In Pat's editor's defense, the waning 1986 was a troubling time for publishing. Federal laws had changed. Any media company with enough money could buy any other media company. Monopolies could form. The Germans had gotten into the game, buying, among other things, Bantam. Bantam was both Pat's publisher and Pat's editor's employer. Now, they were all owned by Bertlesmann, a company also known for being the largest publisher of Nazi propaganda during the Third Reich.

In the true top-down fashion that had characterized generations of Bertlesmann companies, Bantam hired a new executive to clean things up. He often slammed his fist against the table at editorial meetings. His arms flailed when he spoke passionately. His long bangs were known to come loose amidst marketing rants. Only after all his sweat and spit had been expunged would he comb the long bangs back into a neat, pomaded center part.

The last of the renegade editors, the ones who remembered an age of publishing before it was consumed by cookbooks and celebrity memoirs and pulp, stood up to the executive. Pat's editor was among them. She brushed away his insistence on authors yielding a fifteen-percent profit margin with the same vigor she brushed the executive's hand off her skirt.

As the eggnog flowed in the Bantam offices, as faces turned pink and noses red, as simple office flirtations turned into complicated actions, the executive came to celebrate with the same vigor he used to rule the office. He danced too closely with secretaries. His hands sought purchase in lecherous gropes.

The happy executive was as troublesome as the tyrannical one.

One of the female editors upon whom the executive made passes lured him into a precarious place. This female editor was not Pat's editor. She was instead a young Columbia alumnus with ambitions as large as her shoulder pads.

She dangled mistletoe over her helmet of hair and winked in the specific direction of the executive. The executive bopped over to her in a dance that resembled a one-man conga line. The young editor channeled her laughs into a smile. She nodded toward a spacious closet. The executive danced inside alone. The young editor locked the door behind him.

The closet door muffled the executive's cries of

shenanigans.

Without him, the holiday party stepped into a new gear. Reverie abounded among streamers and cubicles. Someone slid Clarence Carter's "Backdoor Santa" into the cassette player of the boom-box. The song drowned out the executive's pounding on the closet door.

Everyone danced: some on the floor, some on desks, some on unread manuscripts, some on each other in the copy room.

Because Pat was not there, she could not verify Sammy's presence in that Bantam office. In her mind's eye, Sammy was there, dressed entirely in white, a white turban decorated with pentangles on his head and a large cigar in his mouth. He walked around the editorial offices in a funny, crook-backed way, alternately spewing rum, tossing handfuls of cornmeal into the radiators, and issuing clouds of cigar smoke. A woman in a full white skirt with many petticoats, a white ruffled overblouse, and many strings of glass beads, seeds, and seed pods danced behind Sammy. Her hair was tucked under a white bandanna covered with signs and symbols.

In time, the executive reduced his banging to three rhythmic bangs followed by a silence. Pat's editor screamed, "Everyone, pipe down!"

Someone turned off the boom-box. Dancing stopped.

Pat's editor listened to the beat of the executive's pounding. Bam. Bam. Bam. Silence. Bam. Bam. Bam. She filled in the silence with song. It went something like this:

Bam. Bam. Bam.

"Silver Bells."

Bam. Bam. Bam.

"Silver Bells."

Bam. Bam. Bam.

"It's Christmastime in the city."

Before she could reach any kind of verse or even complete the chorus, the executive stopped pounding. The silence became too loud. Pat's editor opened the closet door. The executive stepped outside and said, "You're all fired. All of your projects are dead."

Because Pat's previous novel had been a major critical success and a minor financial one, the executive did not completely kill this novel. Instead, he sent it over to Bantam's Spectra line. Though the book was neither fantasy nor science fiction, it was marketed as such. Pat saw her *Strange Toys* in the windows of airport bookstores and under the rolling papers in Los Angeles newsstands. The critics still loved it. Diane Wakoski professed a desire to live entirely in Pat's imagination. *The Los Angeles Times* declared it a vessel of zeitgeist and used it to find meaning in the Iran-Contra hearings. And, of course, in the final act solidifying its doom, it won that year's Philip K. Dick Award.

After the Philip K. Dick Award, publishers insisted on more science fiction from Pat. Since she hadn't written science fiction to begin with, she could not write more. For Pat, science fiction was little more than Albert Einstein's hair.

Pat looked at the publishing industry, at all their activity, and said, "Naw. This isn't the human race."

She returned to her home office and wrote novels, one after the other until they were stacked like firewood for an arctic winter. Art, Pat decided, was what she did for herself. When the novels numbered too many, when they collected at her feet like so many swords on a Tarot deck, she decided to write bigger novels.

She embarked on an opus about Lewis Carroll and the Rossettis. For more than a decade, the Pre-Raphaelites haunted her. It was a pleasant haunting.

Now, eight hundred pages into her opus on the Pre-Raphaelites, the face of Dante Gabriel Rossetti haunts Pat. The Tarot deck that, for so long comforted and guided her, slithers in the high grass of her subconscious. Among the ramparts of brown bags in her home office, she finds the ukulele that can help her through this. He sits alone. The grain of his wood has grown darker with the years, but it still looks like the short fur of a pug. He pouts, put out by his years under the geological strata of Pat's office. Pat scoops him up anyway. He's too cute to stay mad for long.

The high priestess of Pat's coven had given vague instructions: *revisit the past long enough to find that lost source of comfort, then release the past. Fare forward.*

Pat takes her ukulele outside. They sit together in a chaise longue. Stars are hard to find in this inland valley east of Los Angeles. The moon grows ever rounder, ever oranger. It is too large to be innocent.

In a sad and sweet minor key, the ukulele sings the source of Pat's dilemma. The problem is not Dante Gabriel Rossetti but that her friend, a fellow writer with whom Pat had been discussing her Rossetti novel, decided to write a Rossetti novel of his own. It was shorter and shallower, language thin and hollow as the reeds along a drainage ditch. But it was finished first and published and of course became a best-seller. He told Pat not to worry, that her novel would be different than his. Pat's ukulele sings the words that Pat keeps asking herself:

How could he?

Pat's publisher has told her not to worry. He assures Pat that her book will be better. The ukulele knows like Pat knows that this publisher is little comfort. While there will be no big German takeover of his publishing company and no editor will lock him in a closet, it's because Pat's publisher is too small for media giants to notice under their toes; too small for editors, even. He works alone in the back of his cluttered two-bedroom apartment, serenaded by the screams from the speed dealer next door.

His talents lie somewhere outside of publishing.

He's told Pat that her writer friend is nothing but a Patricia Geary clone with needlessly complex plots. Pat's ukulele knows better. He sings:

We need no consolation prizes.

Without moving from the chaise longue, Pat and her ukulele travel back through the night, passing from wherever they've been to wherever they're going.

The ukulele nuzzles up against Pat's shoulder and the heat from his song is one kind of cure.

And so is the sun, soon to rise.

Encouraged, she keeps traveling on.

The Five-Cornered Square

1.

Dick ushered in a surprise visitor, a tall, blond man in a gray flannel suit. His hair was slick with pomade, the back of his neck still pink from a barber's razor. "Chester," Dick said, "this is David Schine."

Chet neither stood nor offered a hand to shake. He greeted the blond man with only the slightest of head nods. Schine and Dick Wright both remained standing on the bare wooden floor. Only open space separated them. From where Chet sat, he could see through that open space and onto the modernist painting hanging on the old white plaster wall.

Schine was only interested in Dick. Without preamble, he said, "What do you know about a man named Randall Jarrell?"

"That you think he's a communist," Dick said. "And you think I know him."

Schine's eyes widened. He reached inside his jacket.

Chet hadn't noticed any conspicuous lumps under Schine's wide lapels, but he wasn't taking any chances. He slid a switch-blade out of pocket and held it in his thick hand. The switch-blade's hinge twinkled in the Parisian light pouring in through the window.

Schine's hand emerged from the coat again, holding only a notepad and pen. "So you do know this Jarrell?"

"I didn't say that," Dick said. "I only said that you thought I did."

"We have information from several sources that Jarrell had been a member of the John Walter Reed Club. Ever see him there?"

"I was never a member of that club," Dick said.

For the first time, Schine turned to Chet. "What about you? You a communist? Were you part of the John Walter Reed Club? Do you know Randall Jarrell?"

Chet's thumb gently caressed his switch-blade casing. He stared at Schine's green eyes and said nothing.

"What's your name again, boy?" Schine asked.

"It's not boy." Chet flipped open the switch-blade and scratched along his jaw line with the dull side. "And this isn't America, you fay mother-raper."

Dick laughed in his big, magnanimous way. "Well, now."

Schine's ears flushed from pink to burning red. "Are you threatening me? Are you nigger commies threatening me? Do you have any idea who you're talking to?"

It was such a white remark. Chet had done his seven and a half years in the Ohio State Penitentiary. He'd lived through riots and fires and rapes on the inside. This G-man dandy was nothing to him. He let the afternoon light dance off his blade.

Schine continued his rant. "We had Langston Hughes on the floor of Congress. He said he regretted his un-American activities. He sat right there next to his lawyer, like a good nigger, and told us all what a commie piece of shit he'd been. If we can do that to Langston Hughes, what do you think we can do to you?" Schine pointed at Dick Wright. "Do you think you're Langston Hughes?" He pointed at Chet Himes. "Do you think you're Langston Hughes?"

Chet shifted in his seat as if to stand. Dick stepped forward and placed a gentle hand on the broad, padded shoulder of Schine's suit. Schine twitched under the touch. "David," Dick said. "I've written all I have to say about my communist affiliations. That's all you're going to get from me. Now you better move along before Chester puts that blade in you and we all end up sorry."

Schine huffed through his nose but kept his teeth clenched. His whole face had turned a burning red. His blond hair poked out of his scalp like sparks coming off a fire. Dick steered him back toward the dining room and the front door of the flat. Schine didn't resist.

At the door, Dick said, "If you genuinely want to know what a communist is, David, you should read Chester's novel *Lonely Crusade*. You might learn something."

Schine jotted down the title in his notebook. "What you should really do," he said, "is refresh your memory about Jarrell."

Dick pushed Schine out the front door with enough force to make sure he got out but not enough force to topple him. "You stupid son of a bitch," Dick said. "You think you can threaten me." He shut the door behind.

When Dick made it back into the living room, Chet just looked at him. He said nothing.

Later that afternoon, Richard Wright and Chester Himes met James Baldwin on the terrace of Les Deux Magots in the Latin Quarter of Paris. Baldwin sat with his legs crossed, nursing a small cup of coffee. His round black face was glistening like an eight-ball. He wore a beige gabardine suit and no hat over kinky tufts of hair a few weeks overdue for barber's shears. A smoldering fire lay just beneath the surface of his muddy brown eyes, ready to flame into a blaze.

Without greeting Baldwin or introducing Chet, Dick called out, "Garçon."

The waiter affected an air of apathy while leaving his post and setting a course straight for Dick.

"Two whiskeys," he said, and only then turned to Baldwin. "And what are you drinking?"

"Coffee," Baldwin said.

"Better make that three whiskeys," Dick said.

The waiter glided back toward the bar. Dick grabbed a chair at Baldwin's table and swung it under him. He waved a finger between Baldwin and Chester. By way of introduction, he said, "Chet, Jimmy. Jimmy, Chet."

Baldwin stood from his chair and offered Chet a hand. "James, please," Baldwin said. "Not Jimmy."

Chet shook his hand and took a seat.

"You know about Baldwin?" Dick asked Chet.

"We have a friend in common," Chet said.

"Who? Me?" Dick asked.

"Well, then, we have two friends in common. An old college friend of mine from Columbus, Jesse Jackson. Left a wife and kids in Ohio to go to Greenwich Village and write children's books."

"Sure," Baldwin said. "I know Jesse."

"But do you know this mother-raper across the table?" Dick asked Chet. "This Jimmy Baldwin of Harlem, New York?"

Chet shook his head.

Dick went on. "Then I'll tell you. This little punk come to me and tell me he want to write a novel about God and the black man. I get him eighteen hundred dollars from Harper & Brothers to type that damn thing up. But the money run out before he finish, so I get him another nine hundred. I even pass it on to my editor over there at Harper & Brothers. Edward Aswell. You remember this, Jimmy?"

Baldwin shifted in his seat. He lifted a spoon and dropped it in an empty mug. The porcelain and metal clinked. "Please," Baldwin said. "It's James."

The waiter arrived with three whiskeys. Chet ordered a second for himself before the waiter could leave the table. Whiskey was rare in Paris in these post-war days. Chet had learned how to drink gin or brandy as a substitute. But Dick was on fire this afternoon. He'd brought Chet along as a witness to his performance as the big man on the Left Bank, the king of the soul brothers in the Latin Quarter. That meant Dick would have to pay for the big man drinks. Chet downed his whiskey and tuned back into the conversation.

"Then did you see the second time he attacked me, in *New Directions*?" Dick asked.

"I read it," Chet said. Baldwin's essay had been published back-to-back with one by another young black writer, Richard Gibson, who'd used his platform to attack Chet.

"And now this punk mother-raper has the nerve to call me and ask to borrow five thousand francs. If he pays me back for the first twenty-seven hundred dollars by writing essay after essay attacking me, how's this ungrateful son of a bitch going to repay my five thousand francs?" Dick turned and addressed Baldwin directly for the first time. "What the fuck do you have to say for yourself, Jimmy?"

As it turned out, Baldwin had plenty to say for himself. "First off, it's James, not Jimmy. You good and goddamn well know that, Dick. Second off, you fucked it up for the rest of us. Chester. Me. All these soul brothers up and down the Latin Quarter and in Harlem and across the States. You wrote my story in *Black Boy*," Baldwin said. "You wrote every black boy's story. You didn't leave anything for me or any other black writer to write about."

A large group of American expatriates and French artists joined the trio of writers at their table on the terrace. They'd recently left a cocktail party that Chet and Dick had waved off for this confrontation with Baldwin. Dick and Baldwin filled in the expats and artists on the argument. A few took Dick's side. Most, seeing Baldwin so young and small and vulnerable, sitting like a trapped mouse to Dick's big cat, took Baldwin's side. Chet drank whiskey and stared across Rue Bonaparte at the steeple of the Église Saint-Germain de Prés. The white bricks of the church turned a burnt orange in the waning sunlight. Chet lost the flow of the conversation.

When the waiter was too slow with his next whiskey, Chet wandered into the café. A house band had just finished their set. They sat around the stage waiting for plaudits that would never come. Chet himself had hardly heard them over the street sounds on Boulevard Saint-Germain and the din of expats, artists, and writers arguing over The Negro Problem. He approached the band and tried out his French. "*Je suis très content de vous avoir.*"

The tenor sax player turned to his band mates and said something. Chet could only make out the words "*américains noires.*" This set his hackles up. The sax player turned to Chet. The warm smile lighting his thin pale face and the twinkle in his deep-set blue eyes squared it. "You must forgive an uncultured Frenchman such as myself, but I do not understand English so well."

Chet didn't try his French any more that night. "What is it you said about *américains noires?*"

The sax player ran a finger along the cuff of his baggy trousers. "We only wondered if all *américains noires* spoke such English?"

Before Chet could answer, all of the band members shot

out questions.

"Are you from Harlem?" the drummer asked.

"Are you an American artist? Are you famous?" the bass player asked.

"Are you a GI still here? We want American GIs to go home," the drummer said.

"What instrument do you play?" the sax player asked.

"Do you know crimes? Can you teach us crimes of Harlem?" the pianist asked. The rest of the band nodded in agreement. This was the core of the issue, the question that needed answering.

Chet raised his forefinger to the waiter. Enough whiskeys had flowed from the bar at Les Deux Magots for the waiter to get the order and assign a tab for it.

"Do you want to learn greatest con running through Harlem?" Chester asked.

The band gathered around him as if he were a microphone at a recording session, eyes alight.

"It will cost you," Chet said. "Five thousand francs."

The band members alternately reached into their pockets, each individually excavating dust and lint and nary a franc.

The sax player jumped onto the stage, rustled through some gear, and came back with a small instrument in a black case. "We are short of cash this month," he said. "But we can trade you this ukulele for a story. It's worth five thousand francs at any pawn shop."

Chet slid the ukulele under his seat. He reached into

his wallet, flipped through several thousand-franc notes, and found an American ten-dollar bill. He showed the bill to the band. "First, you get one of these and one American hundred-dollar bill. Then you get a mark. A real dope. You tell him American bills have a special chemical makeup. You can raise a ten-dollar bill up to a hundred-dollar one. You bring him to a flat that's not your own. The flat has to have an oven. This is important. Another one of you has to act like a scientist. When the mark comes to your flat, wrap the ten-dollar bill in a tube, like American toilet paper comes in. Put that tube into the oven. Wait five minutes, then reach into the oven and pull out a different tube, one that you put in there earlier with the hundred-dollar bill. Show him that. He'll believe that you can raise tens into hundreds. Then you tell the mark to gather up as many ten-dollar bills as he can. When he comes back, you put all his tens into tubes and into the oven. While you're waiting, a third guy comes in, claims to be an American from the treasury department. The two of you run. The third guy catches the mark, gets him to bribe his way out of the fix, then lets him run. Next thing you know, you'll have an oven full of ten-dollar bills and a nice bribe to go with it. The mark will be none the wiser."

"And then you cook the tens into hundreds?" the drummer asked.

"A hundred is fifty thousand francs," the bass player said. "If you take them over to Pops on the Champs-Elysées."

"No. You don't cook the tens," Chet said. "You keep

them. It's a con."

"I didn't know you could raise American tens into hundreds. Where do we find the scientist?" the pianist asked.

"It's just a chemical, *oui*?" the sax player asked.

"No. It's a con," Chet said.

"What chemical is it?" the drummer asked.

"Does everyone in *Les Etats Unis* know this trick, or only the people in Harlem?" the pianist asked.

"You have to know the chemical," the bass player said. "What's the chemical?"

Chet pulled his new ukulele from under the chair and tucked it under his arm. "Mix baking soda and vinegar," he said. "Shake it up in a bottle first." He stood and patted the sax player on his shoulder. "So long, my friends."

Back on the terrace, the crowd had broken up, but Dick and Baldwin still fought. Empty whiskey glasses littered the small café table. Baldwin's rage glowed purple. His ass floated inches above his seat. His fist pounded into his hand. "The sons must slay their fathers," he said. "The powers that be have never allowed more than one black at a time into the arena of fame. The sons who want in must slay their fathers."

Dick laughed. Chet didn't laugh with him. Nothing was particularly funny. Baldwin sat back and coughed it out for a third time. "The sons must slay their fathers."

Chet leaned his ukulele against a café chair back. He pulled out his wallet and unearthed five thousand-franc notes. He slapped them on the table in front of Baldwin.

"Whatever you have to say about Dick, you have to admit he was the first American black writer to break into the big time. When he did that, he convinced all of us sons of slaves that it was possible to contribute to the world's literature." Chet grabbed Baldwin's whiskey and emptied it in a gulp. He pointed at the francs on the table in front of Baldwin. "Pay me back as soon as you can. I'm not a goddamn bank."

Himes stormed out of the terrace. He clomped down Rue Bonaparte with his ukulele tucked under his arm, having sold one story and bought another.

2.

Money was running out in Mallorca. Chet sat in his back garden. He plunked the ukulele he'd swindled off the Parisian house band a year earlier. He'd gotten into the habit in the previous months of waking at five, brewing coffee, and writing as the first rays of sun broke through the Mallorquin sky. It had been the best writing of his life. He'd told the story of his affair with Vandi, his white debutante ex-girlfriend. He'd put himself in the novel: the old ex-con and tuft hunter, who had consorted with pimps and whores and Harlem society matrons in his time, yet was shocked by Vandi's sexual adventurousness. He'd put in the sex. His black body, still strong like an aging prizefighter, all muscle and hips, graced the pages for all those fay fetishist mother-rapers. He'd spent siesta hours recreating those scenes with Alva, his current white debutante girlfriend. Alva seemed to lose her puritanical upbringing during afternoons on the

Spanish Riviera.

But for all the joy of writing and sex and even plunking a ukulele under a fig tree, the money was still running out. It would be gone by the end of the month.

With the second cup of coffee down and the sun rising higher into the sky, the worst moment of every day here in Deya caught up with Chet. He set his ukulele down. He walked through a narrow path between his building and the neighbors' and into the basement of the adjoining apartment house. His apartment had been divided in a haphazard fashion with this adjacent house. The result was his toilet's placement in the next-door basement. The toilet was dirty and stinking and crawling with dark things. The kerosene Chet had poured over the seat and into the cesspool had only moved the slugs onto the concrete floor.

He crushed them under his sandals and sat on the toilet. No sooner had he sat than the trap door in the ceiling opened. One of the new tenants who had just moved into the neighboring apartment house dumped her trash down the vent and onto his head.

Chet took the opportunity to teach her every profane phrase he knew in English, Spanish, and French.

Chet was waiting when Pedro Canales dropped by for the rent. He'd bathed and used olive oil to flush all the trash out of his hair, but he was still stinking mad.

Canales walked into the garden with all the pretentiousness of a small Spanish property owner. He was a large, middle-aged man with a slight stoop. A small dried face between two huge ears gave him a monkeyish look and his yellow skin was blotched with large brown freckles. "Good afternoon, Mr. Himes," he said. He was very proud of his English.

"Good afternoon, my ass," Chet said. "Did you know that the roof of the toilet is the goddamn trash chute for the apartment next door?"

Canales waved the comment away. "I don't own the apartment next door. Their trash chute is none of my business."

"But you own the toilet where the trash lands. That's the toilet I use. I can't have them dumping trash on my head when I take a shit."

"It's their floor," Canales said. "I cannot interfere."

"It's your ceiling," Chet pointed out.

Canales shrugged.

Chet walked into the kitchen and grabbed a large knife. He met Canales back in the garden. He slammed a handful of pesetas on the wooden garden table and stabbed his knife into them. The blade stood on its own. Chet said, "You'll get your rent when you fix that trash chute."

Canales didn't offer the knife even the slightest glance. "If you don't pay the rent," he said. "I'll cut off your electricity."

"If you cut off my electricity, I'll cut off you head."

Canales shot Chet a look with his sharp blue eyes. He stormed back home to get a ladder. Chet didn't storm anywhere. He already had the knife.

The flies in Deya swarmed so thick they sometimes cast the town in a shadow. Chet sat under a fig tree, though the locals claimed the shade of it was deadly. He killed flies and tossed them into ant piles and watched the ants carry the flies.

Something clunked against the bricks of his apartment. "Alva," Chet called. "Is that you?"

"No, mon ami. It's Canales. He's propping a ladder against our house."

Chet launched from his chair, grabbed the kitchen knife still sticking out of the garden table, tucked the pesetas into the pocket of his white cotton trousers, and ran to meet Canales. In the spur of the moment, he'd forgotten his shirt.

Canales stood under the electrical wires with his feet on the first step of a ladder. Chet charged the ladder. The knife glistened in the Mallorquin sun.

"Pay the rent or I will cut off your electricity," Canales said.

"Take one more step up that ladder, and I'll cut off your head."

Canales took one more step up the ladder. Chet grabbed a fistful of Canales' stringy salt-and-pepper hair. He rose the knife to Canales' throat. Canales took two steps down the ladder. "Fine," he said. "I'll call the *Guardia Civil*."

Pedro Tous, *commandante* of the *Guardia Civil*, stopped by Chet's house that evening. Chet ushered him in, through the master bedroom that cut the apartment in half, and into the kitchen in the back. With the door shut, the kitchen felt like a brick cave with a missing stone serving as a window. An electric bulb burned over the kitchen table. Flies gathered around it, obscuring the light. Alva sat under the bulb, swirling a few ounces of brandy around a snifter.

Tous joined Alva at the table. He was a young man with a fresh complexion and a pointed black mustache. The *commandante* uniform was the right size and cut for him, but it seemed as if it would never fit him to his liking. He smiled softly and cast his eyes down.

Tous did not speak English. Neither Chet nor Alva spoke Spanish. Through a bit of trial and error, Tous and Alva settled into a flawless French. Alva explained about the toilet and the rent. Tous asked her if he could see the toilet. In English, Alva said, "Chester, would you mind showing the *commandante* to our toilet?"

Chet led Tous through the back garden, down a narrow walk, and into the toilet. Tous shined a pocket torch onto the trap door. He followed the light down to a pile of trash gathered near the toilet. Underneath their feet, slugs climbed over their crushed brothers. Tous nodded and left the room.

Back in the kitchen, Tous spoke to Alva. Alva responded to Tous in French and turned to Chet. "He told us not to pay the rent until Canales builds a trash chute."

Stone masons arrived the next day.

Still, the money was running out. Chet and Alva would have to leave Deya by the end of July. The book they'd written together about Alva's war experiences in Holland had been rejected by every publisher Chet knew in France, England, and the US. The novel he'd written in the back garden, under the shade of the fig, didn't seem to be faring any better. The World had offered him an eight-hundred-dollar advance for a short story collection called *Black Boogie Woogie*. He'd taken and spent the advance long ago. When the short stories they'd selected arrived for his approval, he threw them into the Mediterranean in a fit of rage.

Now he had to leave town with no money in his pocket, no money coming in, and no one left to borrow from. If there'd been a pawnshop, he would've hocked Alva's old engagement ring. He hadn't seen the three mythical golden balls since hitting land on Mallorca.

With no other options, he walked up the hill to Robert Graves' house. Graves, Chet knew, was in London. If he'd been in Deya, even this option would've dried up. Chet walked past the high walls grown over with climbing roses in full bloom, through the gate, and up to the small, new house at the front of the property. Graves' secretary lived there with his family. Before Chet could knock, he saw Graves' secretary sitting on a veranda overlooking the sea.

Chet called out, "Karl?"

The secretary turned, but did not stand.

Chet approached slowly, ukulele tucked under his arm. "I'm Chester Himes. I was here about a month ago with my wife, Alva.'"

"Oh, yes." Karl nodded and turned his glance back toward the sea. "Your 'wife.'"

Chet took a seat next to Karl. Sea breezes here at the top of the hill brushed aside the flies that gathered at Chet's place at the bottom of it. Shady spaces under the flanking avocado, lime, and lemon trees cooled the breeze. A date fell from a nearby palm. Chet set the ukulele on the table between him and the secretary.

"Graves isn't around?" Chet asked.

"He's in London, as everyone between here and Palma knows."

"Of course." Chet nodded. "Of course. I know he'll be disappointed. Alva and I have to leave town."

"I heard. Half of the town has sided with Canales in your little tiff."

"Well, luckily that leaves the other half siding with me."

"And further rumor travels up here about you taking a swing at the bus driver's son."

Chet nodded. He had. The whole silly event added to his list of local enemies.

"I hear that many of the townspeople were ready to take up arms against you that night." Karl's eyes stayed glued to the sea. A malicious smile played across his lips.

Chet reminded himself of all his empty accounts. He countered with a reticent smile. "I thought they were going to beat the black off me."

Karl nudged the ukulele with his elbow. "And what of

this little guitar that sits between us. Surely it is a prop delivered to elicit further conversation."

"I told Robert I'd bring it by," Chet said. "Fats Waller gave it to me as a gift at the Cotton Club one night. He mistook me for Richard Wright. Wanted to thank me for writing *Black Boy*."

"Yet, as I recall, you play no instrument besides the radio." Karl turned his gaze to Chet. He had the blackest eyes Chet had ever seen on a white man. "In fact, you said you are offended when every white Englishmen automatically assumes that every black American plays jazz."

There had been that confrontation a month earlier, inside this very property, when Graves had made just that assumption and Himes made just those assertions. Chet cast aside the shame. He welcomed in the old street hustle. He took the ukulele from its case and said, "You don't play this instrument. It plays itself."

Chet ran through some jazz chords flavored with ornamental notes. He launched into the Fats Waller mainstay, "Ain't Misbehavin'."

The malice left Karl's face, but the smile stayed. When Chet finished, Karl asked, "How much?"

"A hundred..." Chet started. Karl rose from his chair. Chet tacked on a quick, "...and fifty."

Karl nodded and vanished into the main house.

Chet ran through a rag and a rendition of "My Four Reasons" while he waited. Before he could start a third song, Karl returned with a stack of five-thousand-peseta notes.

"The exchange rate is less than you'll get on the black market," Karl said. "But you'll find it's fair."

Chet returned the ukulele to its case and lifted the peseta notes.

3.

The money was gone. Alva was gone. Marlene, the girlfriend to replace Alva, was gone. Dick was in Ghana. Chet had gotten his advances on all the novels he'd written and none were paying royalties. If he thought he'd hit bottom in Deya, Paris was becoming a whole new layer of hell.

His main occupation was the search for money. He ran from publishing house to publishing house in France with the first hundred pages of the novel *Mamie Mason*. At Gallimard, he ran in to Marcel Duhamel, the French translator of Chet's first novel, *If He Hollers, Let Him Go*. Marcel invited Chet into a small office and offered him a seat in a metal chair with a torn cushion. Marcel sat behind the metal desk, pushing aside manuscripts so the men could see eye-to-eye. He was a slight Frenchman with a wispy mustache and round, cloudy eyeglasses. He said, "Lucky for me you are here. I wanted to see you, Chester. I want you to write for me."

Chet leaned back in his chair. The metal front legs rose a few inches off the ground. "Write what?"

"I do a series of detective novels. I want you to write for me a crime novel. Put it in Harlem. Bring some *américains noires* to my *Série noire*."

Chet ran a hand through his too-long, reddish-black kinks. He didn't trust French barbers and hadn't cut his hair himself in some time. He told Marcel, "I would write a crime novel if I knew how."

"What about *If He Hollers, Let Him Go*? That was a crime novel."

Chet said, "It started out that way, but I couldn't name the white man who was guilty because all white men were guilty."

Marcel nodded. "This is what I am talking about. Write like you did in that novel. Short, terse sentences. All action. Perfect style for a detective story."

Chet shook his head. He glanced back at the door. It was an old wooden model with sheet of frosted glass. With Marcel Duhamel's name painted across the glass in thick black letters, it looked like the door to a detective's office. Chet grazed his fingers across his empty pockets. "I don't know."

Marcel asked, "What's to know? It's simple. Get an idea. Start with action, somebody does something—a man reaches out a hand and opens a door, light shines in his eyes, a body lies on the floor, he turns, looks up and down the hall... Always action in detail. Make pictures. Like motion pictures. Always the scenes are visible. No stream of consciousness at all. We don't give a damn who's thinking what—only what they're doing. Always doing something. From one scene to another. Don't worry about making sense. That's for the end. Give me two hundred and twenty typed pages."

"I don't have any paper," Chet said.

Marcel stood from his chair, eyes locked on Chet. "You need money now?"

"It ain't do I," Chet said. "It's how much."

Marcel reached into the drawer. "Will fifty thousand hold you?"

"I'll try," Chet said, pocketing the bills.

"Call me when you have a hundred pages," Marcel said.

Chet left the office. He trotted down the narrow stairs and into the streets of Paris. This block was deserted and mysterious, dark and cold. He walked the length of the cobbled road. At the end, he paused to watch the flow of the boulevard, where he was greeted by a trickle of white faces, their eyes blank or sinister. Every pair took the time to wash over him once. The sun nestled behind a cluster of afternoon storm clouds. He turned against the stream of traffic and let Marcel's proposition roll around in his mind.

He'd written for politics and race, for love of women and love of writing. He'd been praised and attacked. He'd been paid just enough to hover around broke for a dozen years.

Now he'd write for money.

As he approached the metro, he remembered the con he'd sold to the house band for a ukulele. He'd go home and start there. See if he could raise some of these tens into hundreds.

Ukulele Fallout

1. Healthy and Optimistic

Richard Brautigan's ukulele fell suddenly from the sky on a sunny October day. It landed in Washington Square Park on the North Shore of San Francisco, not far from the Benjamin Franklin statue.

The first to approach Richard Brautigan's ukulele was a homeless wino. He watched the ukulele fall from the sky while eating a sandwich he had been given across the street at Saints Peter and Paul Cathedral. The sandwich fell out of the wino's hand, occupied what sky remained between the hand and the grass of Washington Square Park, and, like Richard Brautigan's ukulele, took its place among the poplars and cypresses, the sandboxes and sprinklers and tennis balls saturated with dog spit in the park. The wino picked up his sandwich and continued to eat.

A jogger also saw Richard Brautigan's ukulele fall from the sky. She jogged over to the fallen ukulele.

The wino reached Richard Brautigan's ukulele at the same time the jogger did. He regarded the jogger. She wore a pink jogging suit made completely out of watermelon sugar. The wino could not help noticing the outline of her sports bra through her watermelon sugar pullover.

The jogger spoke first. She said, "Did you see Richard Brautigan's ukulele fall from the sky?"

She was aware of the nebulous proposal attached to asking a Washington Square Park wino to validate her perception of reality.

The wino nodded. He breathed a sigh of relief that he had not been the only one to see Richard Brautigan's ukulele fall from the sky.

He was aware of the nebulous proposal attached to trusting a woman in a watermelon sugar jogging suit to validate his perception of reality.

At exactly this moment, the patriarch of poetry on San Francisco's North Shore raced to the scene. He ran swinging his left arm and holding his Greek fisherman's cap tight to his head with his right hand. His Walt Whitman beard crawled over his shoulder like a pet marmot. He caught up to the wino and the jogger. He was out of breath. His lack of breath forced him to place his hands on his knees and take several deep breaths. Huff. Puff. Huff. Huff. Puff.

Richard Brautigan's ukulele sat in the grass among the three, glowing and presidential like it was Winston Churchill.

The jogger and the wino watched the patriarch of poetry on San Francisco's North Shore huff and puff until he finally spoke. *Huff.* "It's Richard Brautigan's Ukulele!" he said. *Puff.* He reached to touch it.

The wino gently touched the patriarch's arm. "Don't," he said. "It might be ice cold like the outer space it came from." The wino feared that the patriarch's fingers would stick to the ukulele and never unstick, as if they had touched a comet itself.

The patriarch huffed. He shook off the wino's arm and reached closer.

The jogger touched the patriarch's arm more firmly. "Don't," she said. "It might be red hot from entering the atmosphere." The jogger feared that the patriarch's fingers would be scorched by the ukulele, as if they had touched a fallen meteor.

The patriarch puffed. He shook off the jogger's hand and stood. He said, "We are not naïve waifs, here. We can seek to know the unknowable!"

Still, he abandoned any attempt to touch Richard Brautigan's ukulele.

The Benjamin Franklin statue in the park lorded over the scene. His shadow stretched over the quartet of wino, jogger, patriarch, and Richard Brautigan's ukulele like a WELCOME sign.

The patriarch was reminded of Kafka, who had learned of America by reading Benjamin Franklin's *Autobiography*. Or perhaps not. Perhaps the patriarch had simply read about that somewhere.

He distinctly remembered a line from Kafka or someone quoting Kafka, and revised it and said it aloud as if it were a thought completely original to himself. He said, "I like Richard Brautigan's ukulele because it is healthy and optimistic."

2. A Kind of Class

Mrs. Derfuss read to us about Richard Brautigan's ukulele every afternoon, just after recess. We would sit cross-legged on the linoleum kindergarten floor, forming a half-moon around Mrs. Derfuss, waiting for the day's story about Richard Brautigan's ukulele. It was the reward for a day well-spent. We behaved ourselves through color recognition, through exams identifying squares and circles and rectangles, through oral instructions and shoe-tying and sharing exercises. We even blew up the inflatable letters A-P and R-Z without squeezing the air hole to make fart noises.

(Q was a different issue altogether. We'll get to Q later.)

Richard Brautigan's ukulele never disappointed us. It didn't matter what Richard Brautigan's ukulele did. It could fight off the snake that was terrorizing a colonial family. It could dress up as a bear and go on a picnic. It could chase tigers around a tree until they turned into melted butter. It could simply be a mischievous boy with a mother always screaming, "No, Richard Brautigan's Ukulele!" It didn't matter. We loved the stories.

One of the boys in the class could not walk the balance beam. Without walking the balance beam, he would never get the check mark next to his name that allowed him to advance to first grade. First graders were all masters of the balance beam. This mastery allowed them to complete all the balance beam activities that first grade demanded. But one of us could not walk it. We stood around the playground of Lewis Carroll Elementary watching one of us step up to the skinny end of a two-by-four, take two steps, teeter, windmill his arms, and tumble onto the damp playground grass. Mrs. Derfuss told him, "Think of Richard Brautigan's ukulele."

This boy started afresh on the balance beam. He said to himself, "Richard Brautigan's ukulele." He took a step. It worked. He kept his balance. He said it again, "Richard Brautigan's ukulele," and took another step. Success! With every step, he said, "Richard Brautigan's ukulele, Richard Brautigan's ukulele, Richard Brautigan's ukulele." All the way across the balance beam.

This boy liked to do his thinking out loud.

When he completed the balance beam without falling, we all cheered and slapped him on the back and told him that Richard Brautigan's ukulele couldn't have walked the balance beam any better than that. Holy cow!

Mrs. Derfuss rewarded his success with a PayDay candy bar.

Some of us troublemakers learned the power of Richard Brautigan's ukulele at that point.

At lunch time the next day, one of us snuck up behind Chuck Ernst. One of us waited until he took a sip of milk, then shouted, "Richard Brautigan's ukulele!" Chuck laughed so hard that milk came out of his nose. All of us other troublemakers loved this. We took turns sneaking up behind our classmates, waiting for them to sip their milk, then screaming, "Richard Brautigan's ukulele!" The results were mixed. Only Chuck Ernst could be relied on to laugh and shoot milk out of his nose every time. After six consecutive shouts followed by six consecutive nasal-dairy eruptions, Chuck decided to go thirsty.

That day it rained and recess was held inside. We played with little wooden trucks. One of us had the idea to write RICHARD BRAUTIGAN'S UKULELE on the side of the truck with a crayon. We were just now learning to write and only knew how to write capital letters. Lower case would come later. We didn't know how to write the letter Q because the school didn't waste their money on Qs. They told teachers to just hold up the O and cross the bottom of it with an I. It didn't really work. Perhaps that's why none of us really learned how to keep quiet. Though sometimes we could keep oiuiet.

I liked the way RICHARD BRAUTIGAN'S UKU-LELE looked on the side of the wooden truck. I found a nearby lunch bag. It belonged to Cherie Swain. Cherie Swain's mother was a flight attendant and she packed Cherie Swain's lunches in surplus airsickness bags. We would have teased Cherie about this if any of us had ever been on a plane and knew what an airsickness bag was. Since we hadn't ever been on a plane or learned what an airsickness bag was, we simply thought Cherie carried fancy bags that didn't leak. I wrote RICHARD BRAUTIGAN'S UKU-LELE on the side of Cherie Swain's lunch bag. While I was there, I decided to take one bite out of Cherie's sandwich. It was ham and cheese on white bread. Cherie's mom added a little relish as a special treat to the sandwich. I thought about taking another bite, but I didn't want to be selfish. I carefully wrapped the sandwich back up in plastic wrap and stuffed it in her RICHARD BRAUTIGAN'S UKULELE lunch bag.

Pretty soon, we all had crayons and we wrote RICH-ARD BRAUTIGAN'S UKULELE on every surface we could find: linoleum floors, wooden desks, brick walls, chalk boards, red playground balls, the white rubber toes of Albert Welch's Chuck Taylors, Tiffany Henderson's white vinyl belt, all of the artwork adorning the walls, even Mrs. Der-fuss's poster charting all of our kindergarten progress. The words looked good splayed across the room in multiple colors. They completed the room, and gave it a kind of class.

Mrs. Derfuss did not read to us about Richard Brauti-gan's ukulele that day. Instead, she gave us soap and water and rags and buckets and we scrubbed crayon off the walls and floor and rubber balls and Tiffany Henderson's belt. Mrs. Derfuss used big inflatable letters to teach us a lesson. She held up the letters and told us that we'd never get another story until we learned how to mind our Ps and OIs.

3. The Deeds

Before long, the crowd at Washington Square Park had gathered around Richard Brautigan's ukulele. The jogger had been squeezed out. She hopped on one foot, then another, but could no longer see Richard Brautigan's ukulele. Too many broad backs stood between her and the fallen object.

The wino had also been squeezed out. He did not hop. He ate the rest of his free sandwich and stared at the pink watermelon sugar jogging suit.

The patriarch quoted bastardized passages from *The Pill versus the Springhill Mine Disaster*. "Richard Brautigan's ukulele laughs at us from behind our teeth wearing the clothes of fish and birds," he said. "Richard Brautigan's ukulele is a dish of ice cream tasting like an operating table with the patient staring at the ceiling," he said. "I watched a man in a café fold Richard Brautigan's ukulele as if he were folding a birth certificate or looking at the photograph of a dead lover."

The crowd grew gradually restless and panicked.

This being Washington Square Park, the possibility hung over all of them that Richard Brautigan's ukulele could conjure up the tigers that once lived in Washington Square Park. The tigers were literate and polite. They had beautiful voices and liked to quote from *Moby-Dick*. They really were fine tigers.

But they were tigers. It was in their nature to eat people.

The crowd feared that Richard Brautigan's ukulele would conjure up these tigers. Some of the crowd would be eaten by the polite tigers with the beautiful voices. Some would only learn mathematics from the tigers. They would go through life believing that eight times eight is fifty-six.

The patriarch added to the agitation of the crowd. He said, "A trout-covered wind blows through Richard

Brautigan's ukulele."

A first grader weaved through the crowd. She wore a lovely orange sweater that her grandmother had given her. The words "Trout Fishing in America" were written across the back of the sweater. She slid between knees and hips until she approached Richard Brautigan's ukulele.

Enough time had passed for the comets of outer space to warm and the meteors whizzing through the atmosphere to cool. She picked up the ukulele and played a few notes.

With a voice as beautiful as a young tiger's, she sang these words:

In Richard Brautigan's ukulele the deeds were done and done again as his life is done in Richard Brautigan's ukulele.

A Place Called Sickness

The old woman and her daughter were sitting on their porch when Mr. Langkjaer drove up their road for the last time. The old woman, Regina Cline O'Connor, leaned heavy on the right arm of her white rocking chair and craned her neck for a better look at Mr. Langkjaer's shiny Ford ambling down the leaf-strewn driveway. A peacock blocked his path. The Ford slowed to a pace that questioned the very notion of the word motion. It seemed as if forward could shift into reverse without any demonstrative change in progress. The peacock would not hurry. The Ford could not inspire a greater pace in the fowl. The peacock knew his privilege on the farm. Other drivers had confronted the birds, coming close enough to run their tires over the long tail feathers. This was a crime that Mr. Langkjaer knew he could not commit. The old woman's daughter, Flannery, prized her peafowl more than the chicken she had trained to walk backwards two decades earlier. Flannery claimed the eye at the peak of the peacock's tail feathers was the eye of the Almighty come forth to deliver divine grace. Regina doubted it. Regina felt that her daughter simply liked the odd birds, Flannery being an odd bird herself.

Flannery the odd bird did not look up to watch the approaching Ford. She continued to plunk away on her ukulele. Regina found the music to be grotesque. It had its roots in old-time gospel and the Appalachian picking of Regina's childhood, but something else had crept in, something Regina had heard vibrating around the Negro cabins on the back forty acres. The kids of Flannery's generation called this music bluegrass. Regina knew better. She knew jazz when she heard it. Flannery's tiny fingers bounced about the strings and fret board. Regina shook her head. Where was the absolution? Where was the word of the Lord in this racket?

Mr. Langkjaer parked the Ford adjacent to the front porch. He stepped out of the car and brushed the wrinkles off his gray flannel suit. The old woman watched every move. He raised his fedora and nodded. Regina nodded back. He started up the brick path to the porch. The profile of his face was a crescent moon on the wane. What her daughter saw in this Danish textbook salesman was beyond anything Regina could quite possibly comprehend. The man called his sample book with the tables of contents for the textbooks he sold his "bible." Mr. Langkjaer never called the real Bible at all. He strolled with no greater pace than the peacock had shown earlier. Neither man nor bird, thought Regina, knows a mortal sin from a can of Shinola. Both of them wear their pride like a birthright. "I best see about dinner," Regina said. She stood from the rocker and walked inside.

Flannery played her bluegrass ukulele to the beat of Mr.

Langkjaer's footsteps, slowing the rhythm as he walked the brick steps leading up to the porch. He opened the screen door without a word. Flannery set the ukulele down and said, simply, "Erik." She gathered her courage. Her day's first challenge would be her rise from this chair. The lupus in her blood threatened to kill her, and the adrenocorticotropic hormone she'd been taking for the past three years leached the marrow from her hip bones. When she stood or when she lay flat, she felt that her life could contain perhaps as much future as it had past, that tomorrows could outnumber yesterdays. When she bent to sit, or rose to stand, she felt that she'd aged three years for every one she lived. The process of standing took her from a twenty-nine-year old girl to an eighty-seven-year-old woman. She bent to stand for Erik. The pain coursed through her. She wobbled for a second on her feet. Erik engulfed her in a hug that was perhaps more supportive than romantic.

Elements of the Old South continued to live at the O'Connor dairy farm. Regina's brother had dubbed the land "Andalusia." White tenant farmers continued to work the front twenty acres. African Americans—"Negroes," as Regina called them in her more diplomatic moments—worked the back forty. The house itself, while far from the plantation mansions of old, retained the thick white columns and broad front porch of a bygone era. An ancient magnolia from a time when Milledgeville was capitol of antebellum Georgia shaded the house. Every noon, Mrs. Freeman, the white wife of the tenant farmer on the front twenty acres, cooked a formal dinner. If only Regina and her daughter were present, then the two ate with four empty dining room chairs. If company were present, leaves could be inserted into the table and up to six guests could join. Mrs. Freeman dined by herself in the kitchen, and only after the O'Connors and their guests were finished.

The ghost of a ham haunted today's dinner. The black-eyed peas had been slow cooked with the ham bone. Ham fat flavored the collard greens. Even the lard in the cornbread contained hints of salted pork. The main dish, of course, was the best and heaviest part of the ham: its butt end. Mrs. Freeman doled carefully measured spoonfuls of the beans and greens onto the plates of both Regina and Erik. The portions, like the plates that contained them, were small. Flannery's doctor had placed her on a no-salt diet, so she could not join Erik and Regina in the ham-haunted dinner. Mrs. Freeman served her a bland vegetable soup. Flannery scooped the wilted collards out of the thin broth with a wry smile.

Regina said, "Mr. Langkjaer, I expect you plan to take my daughter for another of your famous rides?"

Erik chewed the dry cornbread until it formed a paste in his mouth, then washed it down with sweetened iced tea so full of sugar that it was more syrup than beverage. He cleared his throat. "Well, then, there, Mrs. O'Connor." Erik kept his white cloth napkin close to his mouth to keep the corn bread crumbs from spreading. "I don't know how famous these rides are or what they're famous for, but your daughter has shown me a great deal of the world around Milledgeville, and I look forward to her further tutelage."

"And I expect you don't have a chaperone to take with you," Regina said.

"No," Erik said. "No chaperone."

Regina corrected Erik in her mind: *No, ma'am. I have no chaperone.* Erik scooped a forkful of black-eyed peas into his mouth in what he thought was a friendly manner. He had no way of knowing the offense he caused with his lack of a "ma'am." Erik Langkjaer had learned to speak English in a Danish elementary school. The English was an English dialect. Colloquialisms of the American South were unheard. Never had the word ma'am been uttered that far north of Copenhagen.

Flannery, for her part, had fought this battle with her mother many times. Neither side ever declared victory. There was no point in fighting one more time, and in front of Erik. She ate her salt-free soup and said all she could through her silence.

Regina knew about this Mr. Langkjaer, though. Flannery did not know men. Regina did. She'd married Flannery's father. And it taught Regina an important lesson. Men leave. All men leave. It's in the nature of a man to leave. Her husband Edward had left without having to go anywhere to do it. He didn't even bother to get out of bed to die. He just lay right there in their marriage bed, soul gone to heaven and corpse chilling Regina when she awoke.

He could blame the lupus, sure. Flannery would blame that same silent killer. But he left, sure as the day is long. And so would this Mr. Langkjaer. As sure as the pointy nose on his crescent moon of a face, he'd leave. She didn't know for certain that this was the last time he'd visit. She sensed it would be, though.

After dinner, the old woman chaperoned Erik and Flannery as far as the front porch. Flannery carried her ukulele in her right hand and held Erik's elbow with her left hand. The longer she continued the adrenocorticotropic hormone treatments, the more her joints seemed to creak, the more her bones seemed to disintegrate. If Erik had much walking in mind, Flannery would have to subtly suggest a walking stick. Twenty-nine years old may be far too young for a girl to need a cane, but Flannery knew that the hip needs what the hip needs. She leaned on Erik's elbow as lightly as she could while walking down the steps. If Erik noticed, he said nothing about Flannery's heavy hand. He pointed to a strand of flowers surrounding a nearby red oak. "Your geraniums are lovely."

Flannery smiled. Bless Erik's heart. He couldn't tell the difference between a bush and a tree, much less between geraniums and chrysanthemums. He did know Flannery's stories, which was more than Regina could say. For Regina, the fact that Flannery wrote short stories was something short of a scandal, but more than an embarrassment. She would never understand what kind of lady would think so much of herself to think that her daydreams needed to be written down and typed up and sent out into the world. It was nothing short of indecent.

Erik trafficked in fiction. He travelled from university to university, selling these daydreams in textbooks and anthologies. He knew the daydreams Flannery would share, and he knew the first one. It had been a little story named "The Geraniums." And so, on Flannery's front yard, any flower must be a geranium. Even if it was this deep into fall and geraniums never survived that first October cold snap. Even if autumn blooms with that deep yellow had to be a chrysanthemum. Flannery said, "It's not so literal."

Erik helped her down the final step and onto the brick walkway. A peacock bellowed. Erik winced. No matter how many times he'd heard these fowl cry, they always sounded like a wounded child to him. "What's not so literal?" he asked.

"The geraniums," Flannery said. "You can know me a little from my fiction, but I don't tell the whole story."

Erik nodded. They moseyed down the brick path to Erik's Ford. Erik opened the passenger door for Flannery. She and her ukulele settled into the front seat. Erik shut the door behind them and sauntered over to his own door. Time seemed to run at a slower pace on these Milledgeville autumn afternoons.

Flannery guided Erik down the various dirt roads, through farms and fields, pecan plantations and second-growth southern pines that locals looked at as lumber more than trees. For someone who never drove and seemed to lose more mobility every time Erik came to visit, Flannery knew every back road of this county. She could navigate him directly into the gothic past and the hidden beauty. Forget country. This place was a whole different planet from the Denmark Erik knew as a boy. He gawked and asked questions, amazed to find that Flannery could name every tree and distinguish the tupelos from the poplars, the loblolly pines from slash pines, the sweetgums from the black walnuts. Flannery could tell the story of the old white man trudging along the road, lugging a wood box of carpentry tools and Erik could even believe that Flannery knew the old man and that the story was real.

For her part, Flannery kept thumbing through the book of samples that Erik called his bible. She noticed Emily Dickinson's poetry was finding a home in more and more anthologies these days. Just ten years ago, when Flannery attended the Georgia State College for Women, Dickinson was little more than a footnote in literature classes. Flannery had learned about Dickinson from a history professor, of all people. Helen Greene. The very same woman who had introduced Erik and Flannery. "You selling more Emily Dickinson these days?" Flannery asked.

"You know we don't sell individual authors," Erik said. He stole a glance at Flannery. Her gaze was still locked on the bible. In moments like these, when her smile didn't push up the cheeks that were swollen by hormone treatments, with her glasses off and no sense of eyes upon her, Flannery was something like a beautiful young woman. Erik may not have been in love, but he was aware that Flannery was a woman and he wanted to kiss her. Instead, he turned his eyes back to the dirt road in time to swerve around a startled squirrel. He added, "You're a little bit like that Emily Dickinson."

Flannery clenched her jaw. "How so?"

"Living out your days in your family home, watching over your mother in her old age…"

"My mother is not that old."

"…writing these enigmatic little pieces about God and redemption. You could be the twentieth century's own little virgin poet."

Flannery whipped not only her gaze but her whole body so that she sat facing him across the bench seat. Erik had never seen such speed, such agility out of her. He wondered if he'd said the wrong thing, if she might pounce upon him. She glared at Erik, perhaps wondering the same thing. Instead, she produced her ukulele and began to strum a few simple chords. "Greensleeves," she said. She played through the chord progression. It sounded somewhat soft, but she played with enough force and confidence to be heard over the wind flowing in through the windows. She strummed as she said, "Every Emily Dickinson poem can be sung to the tune of 'Greensleeves.'"

And, to prove her point, Flannery sang first about a narrow fellow in the grass and second about a visit from death, all while playing the same simple chord progression. When she started into "Wild nights, wild nights!" in that notoriously thick Southern accent of hers, Erik slowed the car to a crawl and parked under a stand of hickories. He listened to Flannery sing about the wild nights that could be their luxury. When she stopped, he said, "With your permission, I would like to kiss you."

Flannery, of course, was no Emily Dickinson. She would not hide behind a curtain and listen to music in another room. She would not lock herself in her room when a suitor came calling. She may not be the most experienced romantic in Baldwin County, and she may be a devout Catholic, but she would not be defined as the twentieth century's own little virgin poet. She spoke softly. "You have my permission."

Erik closed his eyes and leaned in. Later, he would read Flannery's fictionalized version of this kiss. She described the adrenaline that surged through her, the same type that enables a girl to carry a packed trunk out of a burning house. But for Erik, all he felt was awkward. Flannery didn't know how to position her lips, so he ended up kissing her teeth. He grazed his hand softly across her ribs. He could feel the crumbling bones underneath her wool coat, each rib jutting like the ridges in the dirt roads they'd ridden along. The teeth. The ribs. Flannery's sickness flooded through Erik. Where he wanted to feel love, he felt death.

He was at a loss. Should he keep kissing her teeth? Could he stop? Erik dangled over the precipice of panic for one second, then another until, luckily, the sound of a man clearing his throat drifted through the open window. Erik released Flannery. They both turned to see the man who had wandered up behind the parked car. He was a lean white man in his late fifties. He pushed back a black felt hat ringed with sweat. "Y'all doing okay?" he asked. "Ain't got a flat tire or nothing, do you?"

"No," Erik said. "Everything is just fine."

"Well, okay, then." The old man nodded and started again on his way down the road.

Flannery, for her part, could not stop giggling. Clearly, she was just plain tickled by the whole affair.

Unfortunately, Flannery was so flustered when Erik dropped her back off at Andalusia that she forgot her ukulele in his car. The next she heard from him, he'd taken a six-month leave of absence from work and returned to Denmark. Whether or not he took her ukulele with him is not clear. Either way, both were gone.

The autumn turned to winter and the subsequent spring limped in without the usual sense of rebirth. Flannery's doctor took her off the adrenocorticotropic hormone and put her on an experimental drug called Meticorton. Flannery's thirtieth birthday came with a cane that she would need to get around that summer. One year after the kiss, Flannery purchased the pair of aluminum crutches that she'd ride for the rest of her life. These crutches helped her out to the mailbox, where she found her final letter from Erik: the one in which he announced his engagement.

Flannery stuffed the letter in the pocket of her wool coat and hobbled through the magnolias and red oaks, the chrysanthemums back in bloom and the sweetgums carpeting pathways with their fallen leaves until she made it well into the back forty of Andalusia, to a shack that an old black man had built, that Regina knew nothing about and everyone else ignored. The man's name was Coleman. Flannery liked him because he had skin that wrapped around a bag of bones in the same ill-fated manner as Flannery's. She caught sight of then turned a blind eye to the moonshine still he used to make his money. She tapped on his door with the rubber end of her crutch. Coleman groaned and cursed his popping knee joints and kicked over a tin plate that never should have been left on the floor to begin with and eventually opened the door. Of course, he would've known from the knock that it was Flannery and of course he would've known what she was there for. He invited her in. He lit the fire in his little chimney and set a kettle on to boil. He asked, "Would you like some coffee, Miss Flannery?"

"Yes, please, Coleman." She lowered herself into an old cane chair next to Coleman's one table. She hesitated to ask. Surely, Coleman would get to the matter in his own time. She leaned the crutches against the back of her chair and folded her hands in her lap. She could still feel the crumpled letter in her coat.

Coleman watched the kettle come to a boil, then set two mugs of coffee on a slow drip. He smiled wide enough for

Flannery to catch a glimpse of his foremost tooth: the lower right canine. He reached from behind a chest of drawers and pulled out his latest work of art: a cigar box ukulele made for his favorite dying girl. He handed it over.

Flannery grazed her fingers across the frets, tapped the soundboard of old, dry redwood, and tuned the strings. It wasn't quite the masterpiece of dark mahogany and tortoise-shell binding that she'd left in Erik's car, but it was beautiful in all the ways it seemed so fallen and lacking. Flannery worried that, if she looked up to smile at Coleman, she'd cry. Coleman said, "Play us a song for our suffering, Flannery."

Flannery plucked through the scale of C, eight simple notes, then let her fingers leap and dance across the fret board. It was a song from a place of sickness. A place where there is no company. Where nobody can follow.

The Bottom-Shelf Muse

I was nothing more than watching the paint peel off the walls in my down-at-the-heels brain emporium when the buzzer rang. January winds had been rattling the wood in my window frames all day. They beat an unsteady rhythm. The buzzer fell right into place, like a low-level percussion from the *Gas Company Evening Concert*. My last nickel was lonely for another nickel it could rub together with, so I went into the waiting room to see who was buzzing there.

A young man stood between the window and an old red davenport, frozen between sitting to wait for me and mustering up the courage to knock on my office door. He wore a tailored, bluish-gray suit with flannel thinning around the knees and the elbows. It was the kind of suit that wore out before a kid like this could finish paying the mortgage on it. His eyes still darted from davenport to office door, but he added a glance at me into the cycle. With what sounded like his last breath, he croaked out, "Hello."

I set my office door into a wide swing and pointed inside. "Don't just stand there drying out your tongue, Cream Puff," I said. "Come inside and let's jaw."

The man skittered around me and into my office. He

took a seat on the wooden chair in front of my desk. I moseyed around to my desk chair and planted myself. The low-rent dandy needed some time to sit there looking stupid, so I filled my pipe, put a flame to the leaves, and took a couple of puffs. The wooden window frame beat a minuet. The man swallowed hard and came out with it.

"Name's Candy," he said. "I'm here on behalf of my employer." He presented me a card the way the maitre d' at the Cocoanut Grove offers a bottle of Beaujolais. I snatched the card. Candy's employer's name meant nothing to me. Just another Joe making pictures. His title was supposed to send me over the moon. Studio Executive. Big deal. I'd been around this town long enough to be disillusioned about what a lot of golfing money can do to the personality. The organ grinder's monkey was even less impressive. I tossed the card into my ashtray. Candy went on.

The studio he worked for was in a bind, he said. Their lead actor, a fellow by the name of Alan Ladd, had been drafted into the war effort. He was shipping out in a couple of months. They were racing to make one more picture with him before he left. They'd had to open a Los Angeles branch of the US mint to print enough money to pay the writer to type up the script for the Ladd movie. They'd been filming scenes faster than the writer wrote. Now they were running out of pages to film, and the writer had to come up with most of the third act. An ending. No one could figure out who the murderer was. The writer wasn't talking. He claimed to have some kind of writer's block. Candy's boss had even offered the writer a portrait of Madison—a five thousand dollar bill—to finish the script. It was all for nothing.

I tapped the ashes of my pipe onto the business card in my ashtray. "What are you asking me to do?" I asked. "Be the murderer or read the script and solve the crime?"

Candy pulled a passport wallet from inside his suit. He opened it carefully and produced a photograph. He passed the photograph across my desk. I expected to see a picture of the writer. Instead, it was a picture of some kind of miniature banjo surrounded by the soft light of a photographer's studio. I set the photo on my blotter and said, "Is this a joke?"

"It's a ukulele. A banjo ukulele. The writer got it as a gift from George Formby. You know George Formby?" I shook my head. Candy said, "He's the biggest star of the pictures in England right now."

"I haven't been to the Odeon in Leicester Square in some time," I spat. "London's a far drive in these days of gas rationing. All those V-2s falling around town aren't very pleasant, either."

Candy regarded me with his monkey eyes, like suddenly I was making the music from the organ, only I was grinding it backwards. He shook his head enough to rattle his brains back into gear. "It seems that this banjo ukulele has gone missing. The writer can't write without it. This is yours if you can find it and get the writer writing." He handed me an envelope full of bills.

"When do you need it?" I asked.

Candy placed his manicured hands on the threadbare knees of his slacks and pushed himself into an upright position. "Yesterday," he said.

I thumbed through the envelope. Double sawbucks nestled together cozy as mice. There must have been a couple of dozen of them in there. About five hundred large. Good money for a funny-looking ukulele.

I took two of the Jacksons for expenses and slid the envelope back to Candy. "You pay me when the job is done."

No matter how smart you think you are, you have to have a place to start. All I had was the picture of the ukulele and the name of the writer: Chandler. If I went around showing people a picture of a ukulele and asking them if they'd seen it, the State of California would catch wind of it. In no time, they'd start fitting me for a camisole up at Camarillo. Talking to Chandler wouldn't get me anywhere. A guy who could send everyone at Paramount Studios into a panic over a banjo ukulele wasn't going to do me or anyone any good. But talking to a writer made a certain amount of sense. All those scribblers down at the studios were chummy. As far as I could tell, they spent most of their days drinking champagne in the breakroom, and most of their evenings drinking scotch in a bar. Talent for these guys amounted to having a good secretary. The studio secretaries would come up with characters, plot, and dialogue by the reams. The writers were at their best when they scratched their names on the backs of paychecks and constructed elaborate laments about their talents drying up in the hot January winds of Hollywood.

The writers were easy to find. All I had to do was catch a red car west on Hollywood Boulevard and sidle up to the bar at Musso and Frank's. You couldn't spit at Musso and Frank's without hitting a screenwriter.

It was my favorite thing about spitting there.

Writers at Musso are easy to spot. Look for slicked, graying hair badly in need of an oil change and dented with the ring of a dusty fedora. Look for the gabardine suits with the cheap cut of a Boyle Heights tailor. Look for the ash stains on their slacks and the ink stains on their middle fingers. Look for their eyes drooping from days spent drinking in the breakroom. Look for that air of disheveled dignity that comes from years of wearing a mask of talent with no face below it. Look for all these things and you'll find a gaggle of them perched around the corner of the bar.

I took a stool on the short end of the bar and ordered a scotch, neat. The bartender never had the bottle far away from this corner. He poured me three fingers in a dirty glass. I threw down two bits for the drink and asked the writer closest to me if he knew this Chandler. "Know him?" The writer looked at me as if I'd just asked if he'd heard of Culbert Olson. "Why, of course. Everyone knows old Ray."

A few more of the gaggle nodded along. They all knew old Ray.

I asked my questions with a little more volume in my voice. One writer talking was as good as any other. Whoever wanted to chirp up could. "This Ray, he's a pal of yours?"

"Sure." He was chummy with all the writers.

"A fine fellow, that Ray? A real square gee?"

"Did more entertaining in the writers' room than on the page. Always had a story at the ready."

"A real yarn-spinner, is he?"

"Yes he is."

"And what are these yarns about?"

Depends on the day. Sometimes, he spoke of the booming Southern California oil fields before the Depression settled in. Sometimes about the first of these world wars, about his time wearing a kilt for a Canadian division, leading his men into a slaughterhouse, though the writers disagreed as to where this slaughterhouse was—France? Germany? Didn't matter—and limping out of there with a bullet lodged in his thigh. Sometimes he told stories of booze and broads and the *Black Mask*, scribbling stories that left him so broke he breakfasted on shoe leather.

"So he's a sad sort with these stories, is he? Nothing but corruption and war and poverty?"

"Why, no," the writer nearest told me. "He always manages to put a nice twist on the yarns. You walk away laughing, more than not."

I saw an angle and pursued it. "So he's the comical sort? Maybe tells his tales with ukulele accompaniment?"

A writer in the middle of the cluster stood from his bar stool. He was squinty-eyed and puffy from middle age. His nose advertised far too many veins for a man on his side of fifty. "Say," he said. "What's this about, Mister?"

I shrugged and let my glance linger beyond his soft shoulder. There at the table behind him sat a broad who looked perhaps too interested in our conversation. She ran an emerald-polished fingernail around the rim of a rocks glass filled with a pale green liquid that could only be a gimlet. I knew enough to know that this was the dame I needed to speak with.

Now, in Chandler's fictional world, there are blondes and there are blondes. There are tall blondes dressed better than the Duchess of Windsor who sway elegantly across rooms. There are blondes too tall to be cute, wearing street dresses of pale blue wool and small cockeyed hats that hang on their ears like butterflies. There are two-hundred-forty-pound blondes who run the show and wavy-haired blondes who carry little Colts and laugh a laugh strained and taut as a mandolin wire. There are blondes who sit in the driver's seat in a mink and make the Rolls Royce around them look like just another automobile. There are blondes with faces so pretty you have to wear brass knuckles every time you take them out. There are blondes who fall in love with you and still love you after you kill their husband. There are blondes who will meet you in a supermarket and stroll among the strained peas in baby jars and plot murder for a ten-thousand-dollar insurance policy. There's a small and delicately-put-together blonde who fills the room with a perfume called Trouble, who can lower her lashes until they almost cuddle her cheeks and send you into a world of wealth and corruption, along mean streets nearly powerful enough to make you mean yourself, and she'll give you little more than a kind word and a faith in your own hard-earned honor to guide you through.

This beauty here at Musso and Frank's, though, was a brunette. She wore a white day dress with green flowers and a green bow tied around the waste. Her shoes were the fashionable Tippecanoe, which looked like green moccasins coming and going, but looked like sandals when she stopped and gave you a gander of the middle. She crossed her legs and let one Tippecanoe dangle loose off her heel. She was the kind of woman who learned to hold her own anywhere she walked, be it a San Pedro public school or a typing pool or a Paramount screening room. She had the look of a secretary who can only exist in that flawed-fantasy-come-true which is Hollywood, where a lack of imagination project-ed onto a giant screen can create an industry with enough wealth to put an illuminated pool in every backyard. I car-ried my scotch to her table and sat opposite her.

"If I don't miss my guess," I said, "you're one of those Paramount secretaries who does all the real writing on pic-tures."

A bar light ping-ed off her cobalt eyes as she locked them onto mine. "And who would you be?"

"Just a match someone struck to light a fire under a writer. A guy named Chandler. Know him?"

The secretary exhaled heavy and hard like a slashed tire. She glanced at the scalloped shoulder of her day dress.

"Know him? I still have his handprints all over me."

"You worked for him, then, did you?"

She took a slow drag on her cigarette, then popped the smoke out in one quick puff. "I guess that depends on how you define work."

"How did the studio define it?"

"Apparently for them, 'work' meant taking dictation on all the passes Ray made after me. He spent his days telling me about his old wife and her illnesses and his involuntary abstinence. Does that sound like work to you?"

"It sounds to me like listening to a man who doesn't know anything about women."

The secretary lifted her gimlet to her lips. They were painted a dark red, the color blood gets long after homicide has closed the investigation and the crime is remembered only by a stain on the sidewalk. "Exactly," she said. "Does a woman want to hear about an old man and his older old lady and their sad life? Does a woman want to be wooed with lines about how little sex he's having and about how she'll do? I don't think so. A man could notice a dress once in a while. He could ask about me now and then. Or at least once." She ran her finger through her soft brown hair. "He could notice these curls that take a night in hot rollers to get."

"They are lovely," I said.

She unlocked her eyes from mine and glanced down at the scarred mahogany of the table in front of us. "Well," she said. Her coloring seemed to change as the dim light of dusk crept across the bar. I didn't flatter myself to see a blush in there anywhere.

"In these woeful attempts to woo," I asked. "Did he ever play a ukulele?"

"A what?" Her gaze darted back up to meet mine. "A ukulele?"

I nodded, slightly as possible.

"Sure, Mister," she said. "He keeps it in the rubber room right down the hall from the one you live in."

I drained my scotch and picked up my hat. Everything in this watering hole seemed to dry into dust.

The light of the next morning brought me no more wisdom. I still had a nutty case and a writer blocked. I was two days late solving a mystery I'd learned about one day before, and I didn't have much to go on. I knew the scribbler drank too much, which is about as much of a surprise as knowing a millionaire is part criminal. I knew he couldn't write at the studios, but who could? I'd seen plenty of movies, but never one that looked like it had been written on purpose. I knew he pawed at his secretary just like every man who has a secretary to paw at does. I knew he had a wife considerably older than him. That might mean something. And I knew he liked to tell stories around the writing room, so my best bet would be to sit in that writing room and listen. I called Candy and asked him for a studio pass. He told me the executive's card he gave me would work. I salvaged the card from my ash tray, wiped it gray with my handkerchief, and took the red car down Melrose.

I found the writing room empty and Chandler in his bungalow, doing what, as far as I can tell, most writers do with most of their time: nothing. He gazed out his office window at the view of the bungalow across the sidewalk and its window with the view of him. He wore his shirt sleeves and looked tired. His tie was rumpled. A beige jacket hung on the hat tree next to his desk, alongside a beige fedora and a beige overcoat. Everything about the guy looked a little beige.

I stepped into his office without knocking. Why not? The door was open. Chandler spoke as if I'd hit my mark and that was his cue to begin the monologue. "Hollywood will bleed you white," he said.

"Excuse me?"

Chandler kept his gaze where it had been: on that little patch of open air between writers' bungalows. He didn't look for an introduction and I didn't offer one. He was a smart enough cookie. Who else could I be but some other cowboy with a stick to prod this beast into writing? A weak patch of stale yellow sunlight nestled up on Chandler's papery skin.

"There is no such thing as an art of the screenplay," Chandler said, maybe to me, maybe to that sidewalk outside. "There never will be as long as the system lasts. The essence of this system is to exploit talent without permitting it the right to be talent."

I stepped fully inside the office and took a seat on the red striped sofa. A pair of beige leather brogans sat on the floor beside me. I'd known brogans only as work shoes, but these brogans—with the leather soft and unscuffed as the air of a new day—had an elegance to them.

Chandler kept talking. "To me the interesting point about Hollywood's writers of talent is not how few or how many there are, but how little of worth their talent is allowed to achieve. Writers are employed to write screenplays on the theory that, being writers, they have a particular gift and training for the job, and are then prevented from doing it with any independence or finality whatsoever, on the theory that, being merely writers, they know nothing about making pictures. It takes a producer to tell them that."

Chandler stood and walked around his desk. He regarded me directly for the first time. With his thin lips and horn-rimmed glasses, he looked more like a professor than a Hollywood screenwriter. The fact that he was engaged in a lecture with no concern whether or not an audience was listening only compounded this impression. "So what is required of my talent today?" he asked, though he didn't ask me. "To make a vehicle for some glamorpuss named Moronica Lake with two expressions and eighteen changes of costume. And for Alan Ladd, some male idol of the muddle millions with a permanent hangover, six worn-out acting tricks, and the mentality of a chicken-strangler. Pictures for purposes as these, Hollywood lovingly and carefully makes."

Enough was enough. I didn't have time to hear the cries of a typist who makes twelve hundred a week. His suit may have been rumpled and beige, but it still had the cut of a

West Hollywood tailor. Just because he wore it like a cheap suit didn't make it cheap. If he couldn't write with a pillow of money like that to rest his head on every night, then to hell with him. If some big studio organ grinder wanted me to poke this monkey into dancing, then so be it. I'd poke.

"So what are you going to do about it?" I asked Chandler.

Chandler seemed surprised that I had a voice at all. But what followed next indicated that he'd taken my question to heart and come up with the most ridiculous answer he could muster. He turned back to the desk, picked up the phone, and asked to be connected to his producer. Three seconds later, he laid out his demands.

This Chandler was a booze hound on the mend. He'd been strictly tea and crumpets while he typed up this latest masterpiece of glamorpuss expressions. But if they wanted him to finish it, he had to get liquored up enough to lubricate that dry brain of his. So he proposed that he'd return to his home and write from there. The studio would provide two limousines to be on call outside his house, each with a driver working an alternate twelve-hour shift. The limousines could run the script pages to the studio while they were still warm from the secretary's typewriter. The limousines had to be Cadillac. Chandler insisted on this point. If his maid needed to rush to the market for his next bottle of rye or his wife needed to rush to the hospital because he was driving her mad, she needed to do it in style. I didn't hear him specify anything about the drivers. Perhaps one had to quote passages from "The Love Song of J. Alfred Prufrock" on request and the other had to know the Song of Solomon.

He also demanded six secretaries. They would work in pairs, eight-hour shifts apiece. Whenever he had a thought of fleeting brilliance, they'd be there to take dictation. He called out one of the secretaries by name. I knew that name. She'd show up wearing a pair of Tippecanoes and a green day dress. She'd have to starch it so it would keep its shape when his paws ran all over it.

And, of course, there must be booze enough to get him through the last act.

Chandler paused after making his demands, but only long enough to hear some sap say "Okay." He grabbed his coat from the hat rack, stuffed his arms inside, and fluttered out of the room with neither word nor glance for me.

I now had the writer's office to myself. It was the perfect opportunity to hunt for a funny-looking ukulele. A regular shamus would have taken that opportunity and turned the office upside down. Not me. I stretched out on the couch and thought over the situation, which I couldn't help feeling was coming rapidly to an end. Despite the dusty morning sun filtering through a bungalow window, time had gotten too late to find anything the studio would pay me for. The ukulele didn't do anything that the booze wouldn't. It was one bottom-shelf muse or another. I had nothing more to do than linger long enough to get fired.

Outside the bungalow was a bustle of activity. Low-rank studio personnel raced each other to get things going on this picture again. They rustled up secretaries and Cadillac limousines and drivers and steno pads and portable typewriters. They found producers' hats and ushered the producers off to three-martini lunches with a ukulele-less writer trying to unblock the blocked. They clawed past each other in a climb they must have envisioned would get them to the top of this dung heap, without realizing that the smell is the same no matter where you are on the pile. I kicked off my wingtips. One fell to the ground. The other lingered on the arm of the sofa, next to my stocking feet. I lay there, watching gravity pull on that shoe. I waited for it to drop.

Candy came out of the bustle and into the bungalow. He was still a picture of futile aspirations in his thinning flannel suit. "There you are," he said.

I sat up and slid my shoes back onto my feet. I knew his business, but I didn't let on anything I didn't have to. I said, "Here I am."

"I don't know how you did it," he said, "but you got Chandler to give us the ransom note." He tossed that same envelope full of double sawbucks onto my lap. "That's all we needed."

I stood up and walked over to him and gave him a hard stare. "You hired me to find a ukulele and I'll find it."

"We hired you to light a fire under a writer, and his ass is burning. Your job is done."

I jammed the envelope into his bony chest. He caved it in like I'd hit him with my fist and not a stack of paper. I held the dough close to his heart, waiting for him to take it.

He didn't budge. He just stared at me with those sad monkey eyes. The organ grinder had played a tune for him and he only knew this one dance step. I let go of the money. It fell to the ground. A fan of Jacksons lay at his feet. I told him, "The picture business is just like this town itself. It looks like paradise but the air is poison."

Two days later, I was back in my little office. Two days' mail lay scattered in front of the mail slot. I went through it in a regular double play, from the floor to the desk to the wastebasket, Tinkers to Evers to Chance. I opened the window to my office and let two days' dust and dinginess float out. On the window sill a bee with tattered wings was crawling along the woodwork, buzzing in a tired, remote sort of way, as if she knew it wasn't any use. She was finished. She had flown too many missions and would never get back to the hive again.

The one thing of interest in my mail was that same envelope Candy had given me twice and taken back twice. Now he'd given it a third time. It still carried the same cargo. If I were to be a man of honor, then, the best man for this world and a good enough man for any world, I'd have to follow through with it. I'd have to find that damn ukulele.

With no leads on a case that was chewed up like an old string, I did what ordinary folks do when they lose something. I think about where that something belongs and look there first. I asked myself, "If I had a banjo ukulele and it wasn't in my rubber room in Camarillo, where would I keep it?"

My regular room at home would be my best guess.

When the maid opened the door at 6520 Drexel Avenue the silence in the living room slapped me in the face. Chandler snored on the davenport. Two odd secretaries sat on two odd chairs studying the latest fashions in the latest magazines. A gin bottle poked its head out of a champagne bucket on the library table in front of the davenport. The maid stood by the door shooting me with daggers from her eyes. "May I help you?" she asked.

All the words were in her sentence, but she said it in that choppy Chinatown way. Something was off about it. She sounded less like someone from Chinatown and more like someone from Echo Park imitating a Chinese accent. Her uniform matched her accent. The collar and apron were made of white lace. The rest was a fuzzy black wool. Chandler may well have stolen this get-up from Butterfly McQueen's dressing room.

"The studio sent me," I said. I held out the studio executive's card that Candy had given me. Pipe ash scarred the white of the card.

The maid took the card and studied it like it was money made on a letterpress at home. "Mr. Chandler's asleep."

"You forgot to drop the s," I said.

"What?"

"If you were really Chinese, you'd say, 'Mr. Chandler

asleep,' not 'Mr. Chandler's asleep.' You'd drop the s."

The maid put one hand on the door in preparation for shutting it in my face. "Have it your way. Mr. Chandler asleep. Asshole."

She started to close the door on me, but I stopped it with my foot. "I'll just come in and have a look around."

"Suit yourself." The maid turned and headed back into whatever kept her busy in this two-bedroom house on Drexel Avenue. I lingered in the foyer. The secretaries kept their eyes on the fashion magazines. Two typewriters sat on the kitchen table behind them. Small, neat stacks of paper lay beside the typewriters. Chandler rolled onto his side. Both secretaries set down their magazines and picked up pads covered in scratchy shorthand. Chandler eased back into a snore. The secretaries returned to their magazines. The pillow under Chandler's head collected puddles of drool. I set off for the bedrooms.

One step into the hallway, I heard a cheerful, "Yoo-hoo." I sought the source of the sound and found an elderly woman in a four poster bed. One of her legs was in a cast and propped up on pillows. She wore an elegant nightgown. A matching down comforter covered her. Her short white hair wasn't perfect, but it seemed tussled intentionally. She waved me closer. I took a step and leaned against the door frame. "Who are you?" she asked.

"The studio hired me to find Chandler's ukulele. The most logical place seemed to be his bedroom."

"Well, you found his bedroom. Come in and take a look

around."

I knew Chandler had a wife who was almost twenty years older than he. That seemed to be the nugget of wisdom most of Chandler's friends gave me first. So her presence in the bedroom made sense. The lack of any sign of Chandler inside the bedroom made less sense. The dresser was covered in small bottles and scents, the wardrobe full of silks and frills. I couldn't find as much as a watch or pair of slippers that belonged to a man. "You must be Cissy," I said.

"Who else would I be? I'm too damn old to be one of those floozies Ray chases after."

"He's not running too hard after any floozies right now."

"Wait till this script is done. He'll be back in one of those writer's rooms on the Paramount lot, drinking his morning champagne with some broad making moon eyes at his paycheck."

"A broad? Making moon eyes at his paycheck? Lady, you talk like someone out of one of his books."

Cissy patted the edges of her hair, not to move any hairs but to make sure none had moved. "He gets it from somewhere."

I walked around to the empty side of the bed. A couple of paperbacks lay on the night stand there. I picked one up. A Miss Marple Mystery. "You put this here to torment your husband?"

Cissy shook her head. "I won't be blamed. Ray reads those himself. For inspiration."

"What do they inspire him to do?"

"Grind his teeth to the gums. Pick a fight with a world too cruel to even fight back."

I ran my thumb over the illustration of a dowager in a housecoat on the cover of the book.

"There's a peculiar thing about writers," Cissy said. "They seemed destined to scream into a din that swallows their sound. Don't they?"

"I seem to hear enough of them coming through loud and clear. Maybe too many of them."

"There's a difference between hearing something and listening to something. Do you know the myth of Sisyphus."

"Sure. The fellow who kept pushing a rock up a hill. Same rock every time, as far as I can tell."

"There's an element of Sisyphus to writers' lives. Not that they're always pushing a rock up a hill that's destined to roll back down. Hell, we're all doing that, aren't we?"

"To some extent."

"For writers, though, it's more a matter of being forever doomed to speak to someone who refuses to listen. They'll hear you. Sometimes they'll pay you for your sound. Take Ray out there. Pretty soon, he'll wake up and take another shot and start making noise in the living room. Those two dames will type it up and he'll pass out again and wake up and read what they typed and wonder who made that horrible noise. But he'll get through the script and Paramount will find their killer and Alan Ladd will get away with everything in the end. Don't you worry. But even if everyone sees the picture and the Academy awards him some honor, he'll still feel like no one who heard his words listened. He'll feel like he's back at the bottom of the hill, putting his shoulder to the stone once again."

I thought about it. At least I'd solved the mystery of where Chandler got his mixed metaphors from. This Cissy was something. Typically, my business entailed asking every question except the question I wanted the answer to. It was a way of keeping people honest. Or as honest as people can be. Cissy didn't seem to be a broad whom I needed to circle around. I asked her straight, "What is it he's trying to get us to listen to? What's his message?"

"Writers don't write with messages. Not the good ones, at least. The profitable writers write their messages on ransom notes. The ones like Ray who fancy themselves artists, why, they don't have a message, do they?"

"What do they have?"

"Look under the bed."

I paused for a second. A shot rang out on Drexel Avenue. I ducked and listened to the subsequent silence. Instead of gunplay, I heard the rumble of a car engine coughing up its last breaths. A backfire striking the unmusical obbligato to the desert town outside. Since I'd already dropped to my knees on the woven area rug around the bed, I lifted the bed skirt and saw a black case that could've held a tommy gun. I slid it out, stood, and placed the case on the bed.

"Open it," Cissy said.

The latches were unlocked. I lifted them. Inside was that hidden ukulele. The studio ponying up five large for me to find something sleeping beneath the writer every night.

There's Hollywood for you.

Cissy lifted the banjo ukulele out of its case. She plucked one string at a time from top to bottom, singing one word per string. "My dog has fleas." She did this a few times, adjusting the tuners to the words. "My, my, my, my," until the "my" string sang in tune, then on to the dog, dog, dog, dog. When all the strings sang in key, she said, "It has a false bottom."

I sat on the bed next to Cissy. She started in on an old jazz number. The "Twelfth Street Rag," if my ear wasn't fooling me. I checked under the false bottom of the case. It was carpeted in photographs as old as the ragtime tune Cissy played. All of the photos captured the same woman in various states of undress. She was nude in a couple of the photographs. Nothing dirty. She was nude the way the Venus de Milo is nude, not naked like the pictures degenerates pick up in the back of a bookstore on Cahuenga. There was something unmistakable about the model's eyes, something unapologetic, something that seemed to look right through me even when they were looking away. These same eyes watched Cissy's fingers dance a Twelfth Street Rag on the neck of a banjo ukulele.

I set the photos down and listened. It was a sort of respite in the dirty, sundrenched cesspool that calls itself Hollywood.

The Wide Empty Sky

The orange moon hangs over the eastbound 40 like an anti-depressant trapped in a spider web underneath the bed, the kind you discover when you're searching for sandal on a day when the web around the pill isn't necessarily a deterrent. At least that's what I imagine. I have no firsthand experience with antidepressants. All of my life's pills have been recreational; all of my life's psychiatric medications have been self-prescribed.

The moon and the metaphoric antidepressants seem to match my mood as I hurtle into East Flag toward the country club. I'm going to an authors' dinner where the presence of me as an author will elicit a wall of apathy. The most important thing about me at this moment is the woman riding shotgun in my wife's Honda Civic: Pam Houston. We met less than an hour ago. I can't get over the feeling that can she see right through me. A moment of silence smatters between us in the front seat. Her silence says, *I know your kind. If we had met in our twenties, you would've been my next big regret.*

My silence shrugs.

I miss my exit and backtrack through a frontage road

just far enough off the freeway to feel right.

Pam uses her voice the next time she speaks. She says, "If feels so good to see the right kind of trees the right distance apart."

My wife and I share a glance in the rearview mirror. We're ocean people, not mountain people. It's no great divide. My wife says, "Flagstaff really is beautiful."

Somehow, a ukulele emerges from Pam's oversized purse. She slides into a song so naturally it feels like the song was always there. Pam has been on a Wilco kick lately. She plays "Ashes of American Flags." The ukulele is so cheery against such a sad song that when she sings, "All my lies are only wishes," it sounds like an inside joke I'm on the outside of.

If Pam were to make a list of her five greatest weaknesses, it might include (1) soft promises from new age healers, (3) specters that haunt her femur, and (5) ukuleles.

Eighteen percent of every Pam Houston short story is a ukulele.

Ukulele memories surface like sunglasses and bucket hats in the calm pools that follow whitewater. There was the plastic Maccaferri Islander she carried with her as a river guide. A rugged little instrument that could get soaked on a class five in the afternoon and hum through a Wanda Jackson tune that same night. It was forever adaptable. She could replace broken strings with fluorocarbon line bartered off riverside fisherman.

When *Cowboys* struck, well maybe not gold, but silver

and turquoise certainly, Pam began experimenting with the higher end, solid-wood ukuleles. She went first for the Martin tenor—the legend among legends in the ukulele world. The Martin was a dubious lover. Sure, he'd sound beautiful in her arms. He could make her feel like a world-class ukulelist, like a Chopin nocturne might not be beyond her skill level.

The Martin sounded even better in the arms of another woman. Therein lay the rub. She tried to tell herself that a ukulele need not be faithful. As long as the Martin made her feel whole, who could complain when another woman strummed him?

Pam could. She finally allowed herself that.

She returned to the river and the Maccaferri until it was swept away on the Tatshenshini River in Alaska. More than mourn its loss, Pam had to forgive herself for bringing plastic to such a pure place and leaving it at the bottom of the river. Her crime was no Valdez or pipeline running through the Arctic National Wildlife Refuge, but it was something.

From there, she experimented with a handmade Colorado ukulele from Beansprout, decked out in rope binding. Her fingers grazed the dark grains of mahogany reclaimed from the front door of an old Denver Victorian. It matched her barn in Creede perfectly. In her mind, its songs sung all the way to the mountains that cuddled her ranch in three of the four possible directions. Outside of Creede, it was a fickle instrument. On a foggy day in coastal Northern California, it played with too much twang. It's country-western roots sounded almost hateful in Tunisia. A dark spirit emerged from it in Lubbock. She wasn't at all sure she should bring it home.

When she met Vivian and me, learned that we'd been married for more than ten years, together for more than eighteen and Vivian not yet even forty, she shot me another knowing look. *Of course you'd be a Kamaka man.* And I am. I know Kamaka ukuleles seem hopelessly traditional. I don't want to emphasize that. Tradition or not, when I find the sound that speaks to me, I keep singing along.

On the morning before the book fest, Pam sips her Late for the Train coffee alone in her motel room. She saw the guests in the room to her right loading up at dawn. The guests to her left leave loudly on the way to breakfast. She feels free, thinks to herself, So free, and plays her ukulele rendition of the Dixie Chicks song "There's Your Trouble" twelve consecutive times.

With each repetition, the song comes to mean more and less simultaneously.

Horse carts and turn-of-the-century plows rust under the springtime sun outside the Coconino Center for the Arts. Needles from the ponderosa pines settle into the old wooden carriage sets, seeping moisture, reclaiming the elements. I'm inside, answering a litany of questions that follow the reading from my newest novel. The questions I'm answering could be described a number of ways. *Well-informed* and *thoughtful* would not always be among that number of ways.

Afterward, Pam details the questions she found least compelling and the answers she wishes I had given:

Real Question: I noticed that you used very active verbs in your narrative. You said your characters "moseyed" out of the hall. Did you do that on purpose?

Pam's Imagined Answer: No. I'm a writer who doesn't put any conscious thought into the words I use.

Real Question: When you write a story, how difficult is it for you to cut stuff out in the revision process? For me, cutting out lines that I have written is a bloody affair.

Pam's Imagined Answer: Lady, your stories could use more blood.

Real Question: I came in late. Who are you and what are you doing here?

Pam's Imagined Answer: Get the fuck out.

I'm a writer who has written almost exclusively for punk rockers and working class males. This has resulted in tremendous numbers of books shoplifted, but relatively few books sold. This has upset my publishers as much as I should expect it to. I'm therefore trying to transition into writing for people who will actually pay for books, who will not erupt in barroom brawls during my readings, who will not call me a poseur because I won't go to strip club with them. I enjoy every question I'm asked during the Q&A session because the question I hear is, "Will you be nice enough to give me a reason to purchase and read your book?"

All I want to say is, "Yes. Yes I will."

Only one question genuinely upsets me. It's this: "Do you think the short story is a dead format?"

Good Christ! I think. *Pam Houston is in the room. Show some respect.*

Three people during Pam's Q&A later that night ask her what the message is behind her writing. The messages I get from her books are varied and complex. They tend to change with every reading, just as mountains viewed from the north may look very different when approached from the west.

The simple message I can get is the one written on Pam's face. It says, *If life were that simple, I wouldn't write books. I would write bumper stickers.*

Pam's least favorite tonewood is sapele. It's a cousin to mahogany, harvested off the coast of west Africa with all the abandon embraced by multinational corporations bathed in lax environmental regulations. The fact that most sapele is sent to sweatshops in China for mass produced, trinket ukuleles bothers Pam all the more.

Koa is too traditional, too rooted in Hawaii for Pam.

Mahogany is good if it's on an antique. She could get down with a mahogany Favilla or Regal from the '30s or '40s. Pam doesn't like it on new instruments. She tries to stay away from anything made of an endangered species.

Spruce is okay. She enjoys the bright sound. She'd go with spruce if she hadn't stumbled across Western Red

Cedar. It's flawed just enough to keep her interested. It sounds like home wherever she is.

The same moon that began as an antidepressant now nestles Lake Mary Road in its reflective glow. Stars hang above our heads like glowworms in an underground cave, tiny globes of light dangling on invisible strings. Pam and Vivian talk away. The Civic is vibrating in a shared validation of the choice to remain childless. "Childfree," as Vivian is quick to correct.

I've spent most of the past thirty-six hours with Pam. I've been at that perfect balance of proximity and distance to notice a recurring theme. It is this: everyone wants something from Pam Houston. Dealing with this cavalcade of desires seems to be her primary activity while at book junkets.

She has already satisfied my lone desire, which is that people at book events treat my wife as the full, complex, accomplished human she is rather than as my plus-one. Pam and Vivian fill the night with their jokes about childfreedom. Vivian plots out her own not-a-mommy blog. Pam says, "I hate it when environmentalists get on my case about not printing double-sided drafts. Give me a break. I haven't contributed one diaper to a landfill. Not one fucking diaper."

If Vivian and Pam laugh much harder, they'll have one of those laugh-till-we-peed moments Pam writes about. I don't want to know where she draws the line between fact and metaphor.

I pull the car over at the parking lot on the western edge of Upper Lake Mary. A couple of cars are already parked there, windows steaming from the inside. I find a spot far away from the lovers.

Pam's acupuncturist, Janine, found a Native American ghost hitching a ride in Pam. "He only wants a lift to the Grand Canyon," Janine had said. Pam intended to drop off the hitchhiker at Mormon Lake and point him north to the Canyon, but when we got to the Mormon Lake Lodge, some kind of event was occurring that included large numbers of white men with big trucks and American flags. The crowd was not completely absent of guns hanging off hip holsters. "Way too much camouflage around here," Vivian said. Pam and I shared a nod.

It's an American West we all know well enough from experience. We also know it's not a hospitable place to leave a Native American ghost.

The gravel parking lot at Upper Lake Mary is hospitable. I know of it because of a nearby trailhead. I point out north and the direction of the Canyon for Pam. She climbs out of the car, holding only her ukulele with its Western Red Cedar top. Vivian and I give her a moment alone.

Pam heads over toward the tiny dam that holds Upper Lake Mary in place. Damp marshland prevents her making it all the way to the dam for a seat. The cold, mid-May Flagstaff night means that the ceremony will have to be short. One song, at most, before her fingers will lose their dexterity on the fretboard. She drifts her thumb across the strings, just to make sure the song she sings for her Native American friend will be in tune. It's still solid from her morning's strumming.

More than once, Pam has entertained the thought of penning a country song called, "Cowboys Are My Weakness." The chorus alone, which could be nothing more than a repetition of the title, would make her enough money to finally retire, to leave universities behind, to just write her short stories.

Short stories which are alive and well, despite the cynics' moans.

The simplicity of pop songs is elusive, though. It uses language in ways Pam may be beyond, or may be too distant to access. Language, for Pam, always fails to mean. The exact opposite is the prerequisite for a pop song. So Pam borrows one. She serenades her hitchhiking ghost with a tender rendition of "Into the Mystic."

Faint traces of the song drift up to Vivian and me, who stay warm in the car.

When Pam climbs back into the Civic, she smiles like a woman who has never seen a bad day in her life.

The Incognito Players

There are people we fear, people we dream, people whose exiles we become and never learn it until, sometimes, too late.

Kristiani had imagined that, upon leaving graduate school, she might somehow abandon her obsessions with the author Thomas Pynchon. She fled the long linoleum halls and elm-strewn sidewalks and cafés with communal copies of Foucault's books that served more as signifiers of status than reading materials, as props to gaze into both quizzically and knowingly. With it, she'd hoped to also flee the use of *Brennschluss* in metaphors that, should they actually be overheard by a rocket scientist who knew what *Brennschluss* was, would cause him to wince and avert his gaze as if he'd stumbled upon a scene of spontaneous incontinence. Never again, Kristiani told herself, would she giggle as a drunken classmate warned all within earshot to "*Fickt nicht mit der Raketemensch!*"

It was not until she finally saw the man she believed to be Thomas Pynchon that she understood why it had been necessary to journey here and why, through the process of learning jazz and Dixieland non-standards with obscure seventh notes, her ukulele style had become the atonement for hermeneutic sins.

Kristiani first suspected the tall, gentle Tom of being Pynchon mid-conversation, or mid-argument, really, during a break between sets. She'd stolen off to the barista to order a hot tea. Tom, waiting in line behind her, asked, "No coffee?"

"I don't drink it. I'm more of a tea person." The words escaped her mouth before she had time to contemplate the possibilities of tea woven into the meshwork of her identity: I'm a tea person. Had such a thought ever occurred to her?

"It's not a little disgusting?" Tom asked. "Half-rotted leaves, scalded with boiling water and then left to lie and soak and bloat?"

Kristiani heard the line as others hear lyrics folded into a conversation. Surely Tom was quoting Mason & Dixon. She hadn't memorized the next line so much as recognized her cue and sought faithfulness in theme if not exact phrasing. "There's something too Catholic about coffee," she said. "Only the first cup out of any pot is good. The rest slowly grows embittered. To drink it is to pay penance for that first sacramental sip."

"Too Catholic?" Tom, shaking his head bemused. "And what is that tea good for? Curing hides?"

For the next three weeks, Kristiani struggled to shake the conversation and its role as, if not indisputable evidence at least an extremely compelling suggestion that Tom was actually the man the world knew as Thomas and more so by his last name. Pynchon, never really a recluse so much as a man who avoided cameras, could very well be among this group of Upper West Siders who joined Kristiani to play jazz and Dixieland non-standards in Café Pick Me Up, an Alphabet City coffeehouse where they were delighted to find warm and caffeinated beverages for sale at less than ten dollars a serving. When Tom, upon learning Kristiani's last name was do Spirito Santo, gifted her a San Diego Padres cap despite previous conversations that clearly identified her as a Mets fan because, as Tom said, "We need to complete the trinity," the joke was so forced and corny and obscure that the suggestive became the convincing. The Padres and Kristiani do Spirito Santo. Who else could open a door to a world in which that passes for humor? Who else could catalyze such esoteric paranoia?

Kristiani embarked on the journey to learn the history behind this mild-mannered Tom who seemed to be so much more than another Upper West Side septuagenarian in her ukulele club. If her throbbing tattoo of a muted horn meant anything, then all signs were pointing to the notion that Tom may very well be the elusive man behind what were, in Kristiani's estimation, the greatest novels ever written.

Back at the beginning of this episode, sitting on the steps of the Metropolitan Museum with her phone fading into sleep mode and hiding the message that her girlfriend, Bambina Omnipatri, wouldn't be off work and out to meet her for another half hour, shadows casting the long specter of early evening all the way down to the police SUV parked in front of the hot dog cart on 5th Avenue, the last tired tourists posing for their final photos in front of banners advertising the art of Venice and the Islamic world stretching back into the Middle Ages, Kristiani embarked on an idle engagement with time that began a journey without a step. Her ukulele sat encased at her feet. On this platform where spectacle, commerce, and art drip, splatter, and spray like paint on a Pollack canvas, Kristiani tenderly lifted her uke out of its case and cradled it. One song wouldn't interrupt the bustle.

As a warm up, she strummed through a circle of fifths and into a Tin Pan Alley standard. As those in the immediate vicinity seemed more engrossed in their Metropolitan Museum of Art gift shop bags or Lonely Planet guides to affordable Upper East Side eateries or just thumbs grazing over smart phone screens, Kristiani saw no harm in singing when the song came around to it. She closed her eyes to join the song in solitude in this anything-but-solitary place.

She opened them to find a few dollars in her ukulele case. A crowd had gathered. Kristiani snapped the case shut with an apologetic, "I'm not busking" for the smattering of people staring at her, briefly entertained using the tube of lipstick Bambina had left in her purse to make a sign that expressed that simple point, but ultimately decided against it when she struggled with the spelling of busking in her mind. Somewhere, she was half-convinced, a "q" and a "u" should nestle into the word.

Midway through her fourth song, a snappy jazz

arrangement thick with diminished and seventh chords, a gentleman, out of place in most of the world but comfortably situated in this neighborhood with his tweed blazer, tan vest, and russet slacks pinned between a silk bow-tie and a pair of Italian leather roach killers that suggested his whole ensemble set him back about the cost of a Korean compact car, edged his way to the front with a hundred dollar bill in hand and inquisitive eyes seeking hat or case to drop the money into. Kristiani met his glance and shook her head.

Later, in a nearby café where patrons snapped at servers who hid their submission in timely quips, among plates full of mac and cheese and spaghetti and meatballs that attempted to carry the adjective "gourmet" without irony, the gentleman introduced himself as Flatfoot Floy, band leader of the Incognito Players, a ukulele group who invaded the Café Pick Me Up in Alphabet City during the hours when Wednesdays drifted into Thursdays and performed only obscure and intricate songs on instruments that were rivaled by kazoos for their absurdity. "We'd like you to audition," he said.

Kristiani let her mind drift back to the accumulating texts from Bambina, hoping the endless museum meetings wouldn't kill her sex drive.

Before long the café filled with an early dinner crowd. Flatfoot and Kristiani sat among the aftermath of their snacks: congealing, gouda-crusted noodles here, chicken skin wrapped in waffle crumbs there. Flatfoot had assembled a whole gang of septuagenarian ukulelists. Jelly Morgan-Gould, with her sharp German features striking out from the shadows of her cloche, leaned in to cast a Marlene-Deitrich glance. "Of course, you know who we are?" she said, the lilt in her voice so subtle that maybe only half a question mark could hang at the end of the statement.

Kristiani knew. The Incognito Players were the stuff of legend around the East Village when they invaded Tompkins Square in their hired cars. This was no senior center ukulele group all strumming "My Blue Heaven" in incongruous tempos, no aging-hipster orchestra adapting vacuous pop songs into ironic indie rock arrangements. The Incognito Players took this shit seriously. Their instruments, hand-crafted from sustainable hardwoods by luthiers who made only a dozen instruments annually for people whose incomes were like yen-to-dollar conversions for the common folk—a hundred twenty-five dollars for them was the equivalent of one for Kristiani. They dropped their five grand on these custom ukuleles with same nonchalance Kristiani used to acquire a forty-dollar pink plastic jobber with a sticker of a hibiscus and fishing line for strings so her niece could learn to play.

The Incognito Players songs were as meticulous as their instruments. Most chords required four fingers on the left hand to play. Free flowing jazz improvisations came from years of learning where fingers should and could flow freely. No covers. All originals. And no talk of making the quintet a sextet. There were five players. And so, it seemed, there always would be.

If Kristiani was reading this right, there might be a sixth.

Praetoria Splorf, daughter of a the famed Broadway chanteuse Pretty Splorf who had ego enough to become the namesake of her progeny but too much ego to share the "Pretty" nickname, dooming young Praeti to a hard "a" in the first syllable, or worse, to a lifetime of abbreviations to Splorf, smiled to soften the barbs of Jelly's statements. "You'll do fine kid. Let's just hear what you got."

"Shouldn't I wait for the other two players?" Kristiani asked.

"Tom's holed up tonight," Flatfoot explained.

"He's always a little hesitant to meet new people," Praeti added.

As for the other player, the Spaniard Remedios de las Cosas Pequeñas, whom Tom always called Dios though the others stuck with Remmy, he shuffled into the café aflutter under a fedora at that exact moment. And Kristiani, never shy about uking in public, sought to fill the din of the evening diners with a love song bastardized from the Romantic Ballads Fake Book by Hardt and Negri. Starting with a diminished chord to bring the unexpected and seguing to major chords played down the neck, Kristiani sang:

> I'm just a kook with uke
> Just a girl with a toy
> It's too round to be phallic
> Too tiny for a boy

Oh what is it about
That little Madeiran machete
That makes my knees so wobbly
And the pads of my fingers sweat?

So Mister keep your gui-tar
Sister keep your violin
I'm playing my oo koo lay lay
Like a vibratin' carnal sin

There's no blues in my Jacuzzi
It's rock'n'roll in the shower head
For a kook with yook
A lay lay
For a girl straight out of bed.

Flatfoot erupted into applause, screaming, "One more time! Now everybody!" Jelly lifted her cloche and wiped the soft beads of sweat assembled on her brow. Remmy set a napkin on his lap, more like pitching camp than preparing for a meal. Praeti stated the obvious. "My, how clitoral." Fanning herself with a take-out menu to underscore the point.

Kristiani was in.

She caressed her ukulele along the curve adjacent to the sound hole. Idly, she toyed with the notion of another song in this crowded diner, but a real entertainer knows when to take a bow and step off the stage. She tucked in her little instrument and noticed, glowing in her purse next to the ukulele case, a text from Bambina. It read, "Im stuck here. don't wait up. norwegian expressionism makes me want to scream." Kristiani had time to linger with the Players. They ordered a round of beer or wine, accompanied by the old familiar arguments of grape versus grain, and a bowl of pistachios to work as mediator when no cheese or bread could accompany all the tastes. Kristiani asked, "How did you all meet?"

Furtive glances ricocheted under the canopy of Flatfoot's exhausted "Aauuhhgghh!"

Canada, 1968. Just before dawn. Fog rolled in from Burrard Inlet like a gray amniotic fluid to cradle a small city in the last hours of slumber. There were Tom and the apprentice witch Jelly nestled around a newspaper fire in a hibachi on Jelly's Vancouver front porch. She was wrapped up in a robe so thick and fluffy that it could be mistaken by casual eyes for a fur coat. The matching toque made her look more like a Depression-era movie starlet than an aspiring witch. Tom wondered where his images of witches came from to begin with and cursed himself for letting illustrations in Grimm's fairy tales censored for upper crust Long Island boys and Disney movie posters craft his sense of a witch. A long forgotten direct male descendent of Tom's had been a member of the church during the whole Salem hullaballoo. Legend had it that Tom's great^n-grandfather William had busted witches and doled out death sentences. A little digging into the issue found just the opposite. William was no follower of Cotton Mather. In fact, in his own unpopular tract, William had called shenanigans on the whole witch affair, but cool reason combined with middling wordsmithing has never been much of a match for fear, hysteria, and a little gratuitous groping of adolescent Puritan breasts, so so many Goody Weatheralls were put down and history, if it remembered William at all, forgot to mention which side he was on. So much for those old WASP legacies.

Anyway, this particular witch had weed. Jelly lit a joint from the flame of her newspaper fire and, after taking a turn, passed it Tom's way. The smoke of the inhale dissipated in Tom's lungs and blood just as the smoke from his exhale became part of the Vancouver fog. Before all thoughts scrambled, Tom mentioned, "This is great stuff. I could sell pounds of it to my co-workers at Boeing."

Which set Jelly rolling, making calls, arranging rendezvous, or, since it was more than one, perhaps rendezvi, even getting her friend Praeti's balloon into the mix. The Mounties had been on Jelly's ass ever since so many acres of cannabis plants were discovered in an apple orchard tied to one of her parents investment interests, an orchard in which Jelly had been seen practicing and promulgating her almost preternaturally green thumb. Since the pot's disappearance, Jelly had been seeing red coats and flat-brimmed Stetsons like acid trails in her periphery. Now that she felt she could unload a tidy share of it just a hop and a skip across the old Puget Sound to the offices of Seattle engineers whose dedication to fostering advanced warfare made them beyond reproach, it was time for her to shake Marvy's Mounties off her ass.

Tom and Jelly met Praeti on the farthest reaches of the Capilano Country Club, just beyond the intersection of Southboro and Kenwood, the only place flat and, thanks to recent downpours flooding the course, empty enough to get a balloon weighted with four hippies and their weight-equivalent in sticky buds airborne. Praeti arranged her luggage into piles of ballast bags filled with sand and ready to be jettisoned during flight and empty tote bags—long since fashionable—to be filled with bushels of marijuana once the mysterious Spanish runner dropped the weed off. The waterlogged golf course with all its new and spontaneous water traps provided a moment's safety. The three makeshift drug runners could feel the moment passing. Nothing was safe with Marvy's Mounties nashing about downtown, tormenting every creature looking to get high, not just hippies connected with Jelly but seabirds and hang gliders flocked away from them. Even the sky train looked for places to become a subway. The morning fog presaged doom.

A young boy on a red Schwinn three speed no doubt delivered to him through the last available airborne methods, mail coming from a Sears catalog, with a front wicker basket large enough to smuggle a St. Bernard rang his bell to call attention to Praeti, Jelly, and Tom. Though he could have mumbled the words and still hooked these three stoned counterculture refugees, he sang to them, "Pies for sale. Custard pies for sale."

Praeti and Jelly dug through purses and bought pies despite Tom's warnings that custard pies carry their own weight. "They're like Chekhov's gun," Tom said. "Once a custard pie is introduced into a story, someone's going to get it to the face."

This may have been too hasty of a warning. Praeti and Jelly were already digging out handfuls of pie and licking fingers clean. Tom, who wanted a great story perhaps more than pie, asked the kid if he had three more. The kid opened the basket to reveal a space inside exponentially larger than the space outside. Tom remembered the Spanish drug runner and bought a fourth. As if this fourth pie were a spell unleashing havoc, the Spanish drug runner, none other than the aforementioned Remedios de las Cosas Pequeñas came charging up Southborough Drive on a unicycle. He had a Santa-Claus sized sack slung over his shoulder and a kazoo in his mouth. He blew out a warning like a foghorn. Praeti stashed her pie and readied the empty tote bags. As soon as Remmy arrived, they stashed the weed, already bound in neatly wrapped pounds, into the bags. The labor went more quickly when they noticed a fifth refugee, stranger to them all but soon enough known as Flatfoot Floy, had long since joined in, filling bags and passing them to Tom, who stacked tidy bundles in the balloon's gondola.

Once the ballasts were filled and even the unicycle and custard pies were neatly stashed, Praeti, Jelly, Remmy, and Tom hopped in the gondola. Tom gave Praeti a light from his Zippo to get the burner going just as a gang of Mounties emerged from the green of the 13th hole. All shadows were being thrown downhill from the morning sun. Wind blew from the north, a bit of serendipity. Praeti turned up the flame until it shot sideways and, with a steady roar, opened the silk bag. Mounties grew larger in their approach. Tom watched them through the wiggly heat waves. Flatfoot earned his nickname by staying rooted to the rough of the 14th hole. His fear of jail wrestled and lost with his fear of heights, so he rejected all offers for the getaway hot air balloon in favor of the slim hopes that he could bounce off a bystander alibi. Slowly, the balloon began to expand. "Remember me," Flatfoot called above the rumbling burner. The balloon rose a little off the ground and caught the wind the way ancient Hawaiians once caught the shore break at Waikiki. The Mounties zeroed in on the balloon, grabbing hold of the gondola all around its gunwales. The bag wasn't all the way up, but they did gather speed, dragging Mounties as fast as their feet could move all the way across the first water hazard, where they stumbled and sloshed and piled upon each other with little option left beyond arresting Flatfoot as a consolation.

"Real unobtrusive getaway," Tom said as the balloon soared above a stand of Douglas Fir. Praeti, who suddenly remembered Flatfoot from the previous Tuesday's love-in, cast one final glance back at his big serious eyes ignoring the Mountie lowering a shoulder in preparation for a tackle. She blew Flatfoot a kiss and felt her heart, all out of control, inflate and rise quick as a balloon. The witch Jelly caught the thick vibe engulfing the gondola and remembered to tell Praeti, "Aw, quit being a sap."

The hot air balloon, being the slowest and most conspicuous getaway in use since the days when slug-rustling was outlawed, afforded Major Marvy plenty of time to regroup, commandeer an eight-seat Cessna in Mountie red, station a Mountie at every window, and chase the balloon down.

Out of the blue, the refugees saw a dot in the distance slowly grow into a rusty old reconnaissance plane. They heard its engine snarling and sputtering. Remmy had time to articulate the group sentiment, "Aw, shit," before the plane buzzed by a yard or two away.

Without planning it, Jelly distributed the uneaten pies. Later, they would disagree, the argument spanning to subsequent decades, a couple of them in a new millennium, even, about who said what, who hit the mark, whose pies drifted wastefully into the southern Canada forest. All agreed that the gondola was filled with feelings that reflected, in sentiment if not in fact, ideas like "Fuck you," "Eat my ass, Marvy," and "I vant to be alone."

One pie landed on the face of the Cessna, blop, splattering across all lines of vision possible for both pilot and co-. Another pie hit the exposed engine on the starboard wing, muffling the sputters. Two more pies fluttered into the fog below.

Before the blinded Cessna could limp into a wide arcing turn and buzz the balloon again, Praeti jettisoned the ballasts of sand, turned up the flame, and took them into a higher rung of clouds. When they saw the sun again a few minutes later, they found themselves floating quietly, shrouds dripping, gasbag still shiny with the moist cloud. No sign of the Mountie Cessna. Praeti Splorf adjusted the flame. They drifted away at a graceful clip.

The rest came piecemeal over the course of several months, with drib following drab between sets at the Café Pick Me Up, or in walks through Tompkin's Square beneath a statue of a robed woman holding what, once snow had accumulated looked like rice, or admiring graffiti-ed murals among the streets that Kristiani had deemed safe after long trials and errors walking to Incognito Players gigs and, more importantly, walking home from the gigs well within witching hours with nothing to protect herself but a hastily-stenciled sentence spray-painted on her ukulele case that said, "IF I HAD AN UZI I'D CARRY IT IN THIS CASE."

In the decades intervening between hot air balloon smuggling and the days when the quintet became a sextet, the Players had all gradually reassembled back in Manhattan, though drifting in and out at different times over the years, some moving temporarily to Mexico, Oregon, Majorca, Sofia, Prague, and other points literary and economic. They never explicitly said how they moved from the counterculture to those who lived in one of America's most expensive zip codes and sported wardrobes valued at more than it would take to cover a year's rent on a block of apartments in the Red Hook projects. Kristiani attributed it to the same old stories of refugees accepting the idea of drugs as all the same, willingly trading the mind-expanding for the manic, holding their weed at bay but opening the door to speed or worse, the eighties metaphor of cocaine which, as far as Kristiani could tell in her limited experience, did nothing except make you want more cocaine. They surely weren't a part of the baby boomers who like their very own Eugene McCarthy switched over to Ronald Reagan's side once the seventies had run their course. Still, their mystery had none of the appeal for Kristiani that Tom's last name had.

"You're obsessing again," said Bambina with as little peevishness as possible. Kristiani for too many nights had meditated wordlessly while stroking her cat, a short-haired orange tabby named Ruggles, which was all part of the problem as far as Bambina was concerned. Bambina, who'd been taking French classes at night school to keep up with the gaggle of Wesleyan grads recently hired at the MOMA, added, "You could pay a little more attention to *ma chatte, non?*"

Kristiani's fingers caressed Ruggles around the ears. "I found out today that Tom's father was once an Oyster Bay supervisor." It had come up during an afternoon tea with Praeti. The two had discussed parents in politics among the Players when Praeti dropped this bomb. If they were trying to keep Tom's identity a secret, they were doing a bad job. Kristiani once again recited the evidence for Bambina:

Tom had celebrated his seventy-fifth birthday the same week Pynchon celebrated his. Tom had a son named Jack who was in college. Kristiani wasn't sure where but was just as sure it had to be Cornell. Tom had even slipped from his repeated references to "his wife" once and said, "Mel." For what little biographical information existed about Pynchon, Tom had shared every hint. On top of that, Kristiani piled the repeated Pynchon references. Tea or coffee, grape or grain, hot air balloon getaways, dressing as a mythical pig man for Halloween, trips to South Africa and the Balkans. Hell, the man had vacationed on the island of St. Helena. Only military and scholars of colonialism go there, and not for vacation. Tom had even joined Kristiani once on a conversation about the fecklessness of ukulelists because of their almost exclusive employment of chords, a sound suspended in time, creating an Einsteinian relativity unmatched in melodies.

Kristiani had plotted numerous ways to draw Tom out of his lair. She thought of introducing one of the songs from his books into the Players repertoire. She thought of sneaking her cat Ruggles into the Café Pick Me Up and nonchalantly calling her. She considered letting fall a tattered copy of *Crying of Lot 49*, psychedelic cover still visible under the many layers of tape that had held it together through repeated readings. She ran further plans through her head.

Bambina broke through the late evening fog of thoughts with a text, though the two were in the same bedroom. "R U here" The absent question mark hanging above the room snapped Kristiani to life.

"And where are you, saucy one, not down where you ought to be it seems, we must sort that out, musn't we..." Shuffling Ruggles to the floor and taking Bambina by the hair, rather rudely, and in a single elegant movement lifting her own nightdress and straddling the impertinent little face...

With the post-love-making vibrations dissipated and Bambina snoring next to her, Kristiani finally faced that last auction call from her obsession with Tom. She realized that the man was fine as the man. One more kook with a uke. One more incognito player to jam jazz non-standards with. And Pynchon was better as Pynchon. An enigma who could never be a man. A Figure amalgamated from the trailings of a million imaginations. After so long out of the public eye, no vision, no photograph could live up to the speculation.

Kristiani wondered, though. Does the Figure, the imaginary amalgamated Pynchon, when he sleeps, dream? Are the obsessed like Kristiani his dream, in which all that cannot pass in a commodified marketplace for literature or even art in wordsmithing is allowed expression in the restless slumber of these dreams, ever deeper into tomes that break mail order shipping budgets and slump postal carriers' shoulders? By keeping them ever out of the reach of our grasp, blurring out the borderlands one by one, never replacing the horror of collective histories with any hope more clear than the view through a gas fire igniting a hot air balloon, Kristiani and her pynchonmania returned into the bare mortal world that was her home, and her despair.

The Reticent Corpse

A crisp sun shone on the Naoshima seashore. Winds tore through red rental umbrellas like a stampede of sheep, stirring up the scent of coconut oil and rotting seaweed. The tide was out, and the jetty was half exposed, a jagged edge against the surface of the sea. Whitewashed waves hit one side of the seawall. A cove lay still on the other. Children ran across the slick rocks of the jetty and launched into the calm waters.

The shoreline was crowded. Families gathered, backs to the breeze, box lunches in hand. Seagulls peppered the shore in search of scraps. A lone vendor buffeted herself against the wind and created rainbows of sticky syrup and shaved ices for sandy-footed children. A broken sandal stood perched in the pathway between the shoreline and the hotel.

You could gaze at this picture all day—the afternoon bathed in light and comfort—and perhaps conclude the high winds pushed the scene closer to perfection.

I could not gaze at this picture all day. I needed to return to my hotel room and prepare for my lunch meeting with the notoriously inaccessible author, Yoko Ogawa.

My boxer shorts went missing. I don't know why this was the first thing I noticed while preparing for my meeting, but it was. I searched the hamper, where I was sure I left them. I could still picture those boxers, their stretched-out waistband that had, at times, peeked out above my belt and gathered like black flannel cake frosting. I'd tossed them in the white plastic bag the hotel provided, where the worn and faded shorts created a chiaroscuro. The only other things that had followed them into the hamper were a pair of socks and a T-shirt. Yesterday's pants hung from the belt around my waist. They had one more day in them.

Despite knowing exactly where I'd left the boxer shorts, I searched the bathroom where I'd removed them for my shower. I checked under the sink and bed and sofa. I double checked my bag. The room was small, the options few. My boxers had definitely gone missing.

My room had been cleaned while I'd walked along the seashore. The evidence suggested the maid must have taken the boxers. Why a hotel maid would want to steal a faded, stretched out pair of boxers that were thick with the sweat of my travels—the anxious sweat of waiting through customs, the reticent sweat of running uphill to catch a connecting shuttle, the relieved sweat of a stroll from a train station to a seaside hotel—would be a mystery whose solution needed to wait until after my lunch with Ogawa-san.

The hotel restaurant redefined immaculate. The white tiles showed no sign of having been walked upon, much less having carried the weight of patrons who scraped their chair legs against it before standing. The tablecloths were a deep ocean blue. They combined with the floor to give the sense that you were hanging upside-down mid-air, gazing at sea and sky. The sneeze-guard glass separating the fillets from the sushi counter bore not one smudge. The stainless steel surrounding it glistened. The cleanliness seemed to make the sound of a briskly tapped triangle in a symphony. Ting.

Ogawa-san and her dining partner had dressed with a care appropriate for such an establishment. Ogawa-san wore a simple blue dress, one shade deeper than the blue tablecloths. Her starched collar tented around her neck. She shifted her black cardigan as she stood, though it was not out of place before she stood and it ended in the same place after she adjusted it. She dipped her head and offered a smile so slight that it might vanish as the moment moved into a recollection.

Her dining partner wore a navy cashmere sweater and gray slacks. His hair had turned white. He was an American and carried himself with the sure and steady movements of a man who grew up around money. His hands could have been made of porcelain.

For my part, I counted on good posture and an air of confidence to compensate for sloppy sartorial habits.

The dining partner extended a smooth hand to me, introducing himself as "Stephen." We shook hands. He turned to Ogawa-san and introduced me as "Carasuwellu-san." She nodded and kept her hands to her side. We sat.

Stephen said, "I'll be your translator today."

I cast a glance at Ogawa-san and blurted, "I was under the impression you spoke English." I'd been under this impression because, while researching the article I would write on Ogawa-san, I found video of her speaking English. The video was the low-quality variety slapped together at academic or literary panel discussions. Clearly, no budget for over-dubs had been provided.

Ogawa-san responded to me with the slight rising of the sides of her mouth that might, in some cultures, pass as a smile.

Stephen said, "We'll eat first and talk afterward."

The sushi chef served us. He did not take our orders. Instead, he brought over nigiris one-by-one. I learned from Ogawa-san and Stephen to eat the nigiri as soon as it arrived. No sauces were provided, no dipping dishes to fill with soy and wasabi. The nigiri arrived perfect and risked losing its perfection with our hesitation.

Ogawa-san ate with impeccable table manners. She sat with her back straight, her knees flush together, her feet evenly on the floor. She kept her eyes on her plate, and raised them only when answering a question and then only slightly, as though she were studying the center of the immaculate blue tablecloth.

I glanced over at her whenever I had the chance. Her hair fell in wisps around her face. She had nice features—an intelligent brow, fine wrinkles around the corners of her eyes—but she was difficult to read. Stephen sat with an equally starched spine and ate with the manners of an effete who could gracefully work his way through a cherry in three bites. A heavy silence hung around us through most of the meal. Stephen smiled constantly, as if trying to carry the weight of the silence with the edges of his mouth. Ogawa-san responded to most of my prodding by pointing to the food being served, motioning for me to eat. The nigiris ran from light egg pieces and slices of pompano to heavier ahi and salmon, finishing off with monk fish liver and saba. I felt my entire travel budget pass through my tongue and into my belly.

"Enjoy this," Stephen said.

I did.

After a dessert of fresh fruit, Stephen explained to me why Ogawa-san—the author known for guarding her privacy, for shunning the press—had agreed to speak with me. "She wants you to teach her the ukulele," he said.

"Okay."

Ogawa-san spoke to Stephen in Japanese. I cast a glance toward the front of the restaurant. A maid, perhaps the one who had cleaned my room, picked up an ornamental quartz obelisk and dusted it with a black rag. The rag had little silver fish—dolphin—just like the ones on my boxer shorts. There could be no mistake. Those were my boxer shorts in the maid's hand.

Not nearly enough time had passed for her to wash them prior to employing them as a dust rag.

Stephen translated Ogawa-san's Japanese. "First, she learns the ukulele," he said. "Then you get your interview."

The hotel was U-shaped. Ogawa-san's room was directly across the courtyard from mine. The curtains in all the rooms were gauzy, see-through. In the evening of my first night in the hotel, all of the east-wing guests' lives played out before me in silhouette. Ogawa-san didn't bother to close her curtains. I could see directly into her room. She sat hunched over a laptop, battering the keys with the speed and assuredness of a concert pianist. She paused only occasionally, and only to talk to herself.

Beyond the east wing sat a hill. An orchard ran up the hill: some peach trees, some loquats, a few grape vines. The rest of the hill was covered in kiwi trees. During the day, it had been nothing but the most beautiful fruit. During the moonlit night, with the wind blowing, the whole hillside trembled as though covered with a swarm of dark-green bats.

I alternately watched the moonlight glistening on the hotel pool in the courtyard, the trembling kiwi trees, and the rapid tapping of Ogawa-san's fingers on the keyboard. I felt as if I should write something. I'd been paid to do so. The payment would pale in comparison to the time and money I'd invested in this venture. My travel budget was depleted on a plane ticket and a lunch for three. The rest of the expenses would be covered from my equally limited bank account. All of this effort and money in the hope of securing an interview with an author who seemed passively hostile to the idea of speaking to me.

I wound up a toy robot and watched him take four steps across my desk. I wound him up again. He walked the other way. I'd brought this robot with me from California. He was a talisman, a way to calm myself before writing. I watched him pace along the surface of my hotel desk. I struggled to scribble a few notes, then went back to the scene outside my window.

The maid scuttled from the back door of the hotel, down the hill toward the seashore. She carried a cardboard produce box. It sagged on the bottom. The maid was elderly. She'd been visibly working around the hotel since I'd checked in that morning. Despite the hours that had passed and her advanced age and the evident weight of the produce box, the maid raced down the hill as if the box and the burden were a part of her being.

I couldn't write. I couldn't sleep. I couldn't stare at the lives of strangers anymore. I headed down to the moonlit pool for a late-evening swim.

I dove in and counted my laps in the ten-meter increments of the pool. Ten, twenty, thirty, until I completed fifty meters in each of the four major strokes. My decision to end with the butterfly—the loudest of the strokes—seemed to have irritated one of the guests. His derisions echoed every time I emerged for a new breath.

The next day, the maid caught me outside my room around noon. Jet lag and the residual effects of a late-evening swim kept me up late and led to me sleeping through breakfast. I'd made a plan to head into town and find food before my two o'clock appointment with Ogawa-san. The maid grabbed my elbow before I could make my way down the hall. She said something to me in Japanese. I shrugged and asked, "Do you, by any chance, speak English?"

She shook her head. "*Pero hablo un poco español.*"

"*Muy bien,*" I said, "*¿Que pasa?*"

"*¿Te gusta comer? Desayuno...*" She paused, perhaps looking for a way to say "passed," then simplified the sentiment to, "*No desayuno.*"

I asked her to suggest somewhere I could eat. She led me to believe that this was her lunch break. I wasn't sure if she was leading me to a restaurant or if she was joining me for lunch. Either way, I made sure to keep my hand near my wallet.

She led me along the seashore toward a stand of small restaurants. The wind had died down, and the beach was more crowded than it had been the day before. My line of vision was nearly overwhelmed by the red rental umbrellas, fully recovered from their previous day's battle with the wind and now blanketing the sand in shade. A beach ball sailed over the umbrellas and landed at my feet. I kicked it—a soft push-pass—back to a running little boy. A small girl with a face covered in ice cream walked passed us. Couples strolled hand-in-hand, their wet swimming trunks soaking through the towels wrapped around their waists.

The maid pointed out a small pizza place. We each

ordered a slice, which turned out to be one-quarter of a large pizza. We stood at the scratched and worn wooden counter. I tried to keep my weight off the wood and my arms free of the collected oil and tomato sauce and Tabasco that speckled the counter like modern art. A cloud of cigarette smoke hung in the shadows under the awning, and a surly waiter shuffled among the rickety tables. Tiny cockroaches skittered over the condiments.

I nibbled my slice and sipped my lemonade. The maid ordered a beer to go with her slice. She drank it all straight from the can—something I'd never seen a Japanese person do—and crushed the empty before turning to her pizza. She shouted, "*Cerveza*," to the girl at the counter, then clarified her order in Japanese.

After polishing off a second slice and two more beers, the maid told me a story in her best Spanish. She said that she used to work at another hotel in town. She searched for the word in Spanish for the hotel, gave up, and called it the *Sakura*. I told her everyone knows what sakura means, regardless of the language. She said that the hotel owner's daughter had had a masochistic affair with a local man who'd killed his wife. He'd been a translator, Russian-to-Japanese. When the affair was discovered, he took to the sea to escape censure. He tried to swim away. This, the maid made clear. "*Nadó. Nadó*," she said. She'd born witness to it all. She'd even steamed open the envelopes and read the love letters the man sent the girl. They were filthy, she said.

The story she told was fresh in my mind, though some

of the details were off. I asked the maid if the hotel hadn't been named the Hotel Iris, as it had been when Ogawa-san wrote the novel of that name. The maid responded by spitting on the floor. She ran the bottom of her sandal across the puddle of spit, leaving what appeared to be the only clean streak on the restaurant tile. "Ogawa stole everything she wrote from me," the maid said, in her first words of English.

Stephen and I sat in poolside chairs, watching Ogawa-san swim laps. Stephen was dressed as impeccably as he'd been the day before. Though his white slacks bore the signs of being well-worn, they also boasted a wearer's ability to chauffeur white through a gauntlet of food, mud, and inks and emerge unstained. My plaid shorts were frayed at the hems. My T-shirt was probably newer than his slacks and it was black, but a month-old bleach stain was hidden only by my apathy. We watched Ogawa-san swim laps. She doubled my previous night's swimming performance. One hundred meters for each of the four major strokes.

By the time she reached the butterfly, tension had settled like a fog between Stephen and me. Stephen's perpetual smile struggled to dissipate it. I wanted to tell him that a simple statement along the lines of, *Don't worry. She'll come around to your interview before it's time for you to fly back to California*, would work a lot better than a smile. I turned my glance away from Stephen's smile and Ogawa-san's laps and watched another guest, a little girl with the pale skin of a city-dweller making her first voyage seaward, play with a toy robot. She wound up the robot. It took four paces before the spring ran out. The girl wound it up again. The robot walked a little farther. The girl did not smile. She looked at both of her parents. When it was clear that they were not watching, when she thought no one was watching, she quietly applauded the robot. Clap. Clap.

I looked closely at the robot. It was the very same type of robot I'd had as a small child. It was also identical to the robot I'd brought with me from California, the one that had been in my hotel room prior to the maid coming in to clean.

To fill the space between Stephen and I while Ogawa-san swam her final four laps, I told him about the maid and my robot. Stephen said nothing while I talked. When I finished, he quietly stood, walked around the pool, and spoke to the parents. Their conversation was in Japanese. I couldn't understand the words. I could understand the tenor of the discussion. Stephen accused. The parents defended. The volume of their voices escalated. The mother's face flushed a tomato red. Stephen pounded his open palm with a closed fist. The father raised his hands above his head in a multi-lingual gesture of frustration. Stephen resolved matters by yanking the robot out of the little girl's hand.

He turned and headed back around the pool. The parents remained seated. The little girl neither spoke nor cried. She simply glared at me.

Stephen handed me the toy robot. "Perhaps it would be better if we took this ukulele lesson up to my room. Ogawa-san can join us when she's done swimming."

I kept my eyes on the girl, my hands on the robot. I nodded in agreement.

To show off, I played a ukulele rendition of "Ode to Joy" for Ogawa-san. I was using my travel ukulele with its plastic fretboard and plywood soundboard. The image of the small, robot-less girl lingered in my memory. It blended with the forced joy of the song. The music sounded like the rust on the Picasso sculpture in front of the Cook County Court-house. Ogawa-san sat primly on the corner of Stephen's hotel-room bed. Her ukulele lay across her lap, strings down. Her folded hands rested on the back of her ukulele. Her eyes watched my fingers.

When I finished the song, Ogawa-san spoke to me in what I thought was Japanese. I looked to Stephen to trans-late. He said the same words. I told him I didn't understand. They both made the request again, louder and slower. "Liszt," they said. "The 'Liebestraum.'" I didn't know the piece at all, much less on the ukulele. I played a slow rendition of Patsy Cline's "Crazy," mixing melody with rhythm hope-fully with enough emotion to mask my ignorance. Stephen and Ogawa-san sat patiently through it. Ogawa-san spoke to Stephen at the end. Stephen asked, "Do you know any traditional Hawaiian songs?"

Given a few minutes, I could have found "Aloha Oe" somewhere on the fretboard. The two had already humored my performance of "Crazy." I wanted something more.

I played "Papalina Lahilahi," first in the upbeat tempo it was written in, and second sadly, slowly, like the song of a doomed island.

Afterward, the lesson began in earnest. I taught Ogawa-san the key of G. It has the easiest chords for someone who already knows guitar. She impatiently hurried me through them, until I showed her how to find "Ode to Joy" within those basic G and D chords. She attacked the fretboard, plucking mistimed and mistaken notes, eventually finding fragments of the song that lingered within.

This seemed to be enough for her. She focused intensely, almost obsessively, on her search for the arrangement within the chords, pausing only to mutter something to Stephen. Stephen stood to usher me out of his room.

"Wait," I said. "One more thing."

Ogawa-san stopped her plucking and looked at me. To show her that I did, in fact, know her work, that I understood it somewhat, I showed her the diminished chord. Played on its own, it's unimpressive. Played three times in succession, moved down one fret with each strum, it makes the sound that cartoons use to portend doom. BUM BUM BUM.

I struck the chords and smiled. Ogawa-san glared at me with the same face as the robot-less little girl.

Stephen said, "Ogawa-san will grant your interview tomorrow."

Tomorrow. The day I was scheduled to leave the Japanese seashore.

The concierge recommended I visit the town's aquarium. This gave me the idea of supplementing my possibly futile interview attempt with a travel piece about the Naoshima seashore. Something like, "The minute you arrive, you feel you've stepped into paradise. It's like a Mediterranean village with a Japanese twist. The villagers are warm. The service in the local establishments is impeccable. The beach is seconds away from everything, and the gentle surf of the cove is perfect for kids. As an added attraction, you can visit the village aquarium and watch the playful dalliance of seals, dolphins, and sea otters."

In truth, the aquarium seal was anorexic. He lay flat on the concrete edge of the pool, barking softly and incessantly. The dolphin floated in the middle of the pool. He didn't react in any way to the teenage boys who banged fifty-yen coins against the aquarium glass and screamed for him to swim. I bought a more-than-four-days-dead fish for a hundred yen and tossed it over the tank to the dolphin. He drifted to the surface of the water, pushed the fish with his nose, and gradually descended away. The dead fish floated on the surface.

As I left, the sea otter made eye contact with me. He rubbed his fingers and dove, swimming straight for me. He spun in the water and stared at me. If there had been a translator available, she may have clarified that the sea otter wanted me to take him back to California with me.

That night, Ogawa-san left her window as open as her curtains. She sat on her bed, playing ukulele. Her fingers danced through "Ode to Joy." Not just the brief, two-minute chorus that I'd played, but all four movements. I watched the kiwis on the hill tremble in the wind and listened to Ogawa-san's ukulele.

Like the night before, the maid emerged from the hotel's back door with a saggy-bottomed produce box. She scuttled down the hill toward the sea. I raced out the door to follow her.

She darted through the kiwis, well ahead of me, whipped through town as if unseen by the tourists out for beer, karaoke, last-call love affairs. She hopped onto the foot of the jetty. I nearly caught up to her there. Once on the rocks, she was too quick. She bounced across them with the grace of a mountain goat. The rocks were slick. The soles of my shoes were slicker. The spinning white light at the end of the pier alternately lit my path and blinded me. By the time my eyes were able to readjust to the dark, the light slapped me again. Sea spray whipped up to my left. The cove to my right invited me to dive in, swim the calm waters back to shore. I continued to follow the maid.

She stopped at end of the pier, just below the spinning light. One by one, she tossed the contents of her box into the sea on the rugged side of the pier.

The box was half-empty by the time I met her. Below the spinning light, underneath its blinding beam, the moon was enough to cast a pallor on the scene. Her box was, indeed, full of food. Brown heads of lettuce dripped onto squishy tomatoes and spongy cucumbers. Gray scallops seeped out of the gaping mouths of their shells. Lobster heads looked alive with insects crawling among the congealed brains. Old strawberry shortcakes stained their cellophane wrappers, brown cream separated from the fat, strawberries dried and wrinkled like the heads of dead babies, sponge cake hardened and crumbling, mold wrapping around it all. The maid tossed all the rotten food into the same spot in the sea. A dolphin had come to meet her. He splashed and played in the food, smacking it with his tail, spinning around it, turning one spot of the water into a festering stew. The maid continued to toss the food to the dolphin.

"What are you doing?" I asked her. "*¿Que pasa?*"

"*El pescado sabe,*" she said. She explained that she and the fish had struck a deal. She mentioned something about translation—*traducir*—but I didn't follow. She told me it all had to do with the Hotel Sakura—the Hotel Iris, as Ogawa-san had called it—and the missing man, the one who had tried to swim to safety. The maid said she would prove that Ogawa-san had been stealing her stories. She would show everyone. The fish would help her.

She continued to throw the rotten food into the sea. The dolphin seemed to tire of the sandbox. He swam away, or at least down. "*Mire,*" she told me.

So I watched. The wind skipped across the surface of the water. The rotted food bobbed and dissolved. The colors of the mush the dolphin had created swirled together in a moonlit silver and broke apart. The maid stared at the ocean.

Gradually, something began to creep to the surface. It looked like a corpse in a desiccated state similar to the food the maid had tossed. It was the torso of a man wearing a tattered gray suit. His round, bald head hung limply from a decomposing neck. The maid pointed and screamed, "*¡El traductor! ¡El traductor!*"

The next morning, my time and money had run too thin. I had to check out without, it seemed, a Yoko Ogawa interview. I spent the morning working on a story of my time at the seashore, hoping it would suffice. I wrote about the armada of red umbrellas, the slick rocks of the jetty, the anorexic seal, the immaculate sushi bar, Ogawa-san furiously typing across the courtyard, my wind-up robot pacing on a hotel desk, the maid, her thefts and claims of theft. When I finished, I packed my bag and headed out. I took no time to assess what items may have been left behind involuntarily.

"The maid. She was an elderly woman." I imitated her slumped posture for the concierge. "She never stopped moving. Spoke Spanish."

"I know of whom you speak. She lives in town. She used to be a maid here."

"She doesn't still work here?" I asked.

"We keep telling her that," he said in his flawless English.

"And Ogawa-san?" I asked

"She checked out early this morning."

I walked through all the hallways looking for the maid. I slumped under the weight of my backpack. Sweat formed where the straps of the pack rubbed against my chest. The maid was nowhere to be found. I went to the seashore for a final look. It was crowded as ever, umbrellas jostling one another, kids racing along the rocks of the jetties, couples staring into one another's eyes. No sign of the maid or Ogawa-san.

A spotless American approached me, holding a handful of pages torn from a notebook. As he got closer, I recognized him as Stephen. "Ogawa-san left this for you," he told me. "She wrote the interview herself. I translated."

"Thank you," I said. I shook his porcelain hand. He turned and walked away. I headed for the train that would take me off the island, to the Kōnan Airport.

As the train whipped through the lush hills, I stole my first glance at the notebook pages Stephen handed me. The letters swirled around the page as if spun from my own thoughts.

A crisp sun shone on the Naoshima seashore. The tide was out, and the jetty was half exposed, a jagged edge against the surface of the sea. Children ran across the slick rocks of the jetty and launched into the calm waters.

Ukes for the Little Guy

As a small child, Sean Carswell tried to turn everything into a ukulele. Broom handles, armadillo shells, the cardboard box his sister's Barbie arrived in, the remains of a bat José Cruz broke in a spring training game. He'd even make miniature ukuleles out of beetle shells and toothpicks and give them to his sister, for her dolls. The small ones gathered dust in dollhouse corners. The human-sized ones usually crumbled under the tension of strings tightened to some facsimile of tuned.

When Sean Carswell butted heads with his second grade teacher, a woman who began the year as Miss Sunday and ended it as Mrs. Matthews, his mother tried to turn the obsessive uke building into a survival mechanism.

A beginning of the year Miss Sunday nurtured a classroom environment that was very friendly for the slowest students. No question was too stupid, no problem too simple to repeat infinitely. Sean Carswell would finish all the math problems in his textbook while Dave Gast struggled with the first one: 15 + 6 =, raising his hand repeatedly, summoning Miss Sunday first 15 times, then 6 times, for a total of, as he figured it, 156 times. Sean Carswell would read to the end of the class read-along while Caryn Paige stuttered across the word "knot" every time it reemerged: surprised anew with each occurrence, perpetually pronouncing the "k." A silent letter was too much for Caryn's developing brain. At this rate, she'd never learn to properly misspell her name.

Once finished with his math or reading, a seven-year-old Sean Carswell didn't know what to do with himself. Sometimes, he'd fume. He suspected his classmates knew better. Dave Gast may struggle over 15 + 6, but he damn sure knew that, when his Pee Wee football team had five field goals and added a touchdown to it, their score would become 21. At least until the extra point was converted. Caryn probably was a bad reader. Sean Carswell felt she would have been a better reader if every other boy in the class didn't shower her every mistake in sighs and moon eyes. Sean Carswell supposed that none of his classmates were as dumb as they acted in Miss Sunday's class. They just knew Miss Sunday would make them do less work if they acted stupid.

Sean Carswell was in agony. He sought wisdom from the stories overheard in his living room. His brother and sister watched television when the TV worked. Sean Carswell only watched when it was broken, when his father and a buddy and a six-pack of Stroh's huddled in the living room corner, seeking a blown picture tube and telling stories. Old Ronnie Crilly told Sean Carswell's father a story about trouble at work. Ronnie said, "I was going out of my skull, so fucking bored, when I finally decided that, if shit wasn't going to go down, I was gonna start some."

Sean Carswell learned more in this vocabulary lesson than he had in six weeks of Miss Sunday's lists. He decided that he would start some shit the next time he was going out of his skull, so fucking bored. The opportunity emerged around Thanksgiving time. The class was expected to trace their hands and draw a turkey out of the tracings. Poor little Dan Shock could not figure it out. Should the head of the turkey go on the thumb or the pinkie? Obviously, for Dan, the pinkie was the answer. If Ronnie Crilly were commenting on the situation while the Stroh's disappeared and the broken picture tubes multiplied, he'd say, "The kid couldn't find the ass end of a turkey." Sean Carswell knew better than to say this. But with his turkey drawn and his next day's homework complete, with every book on the library's second grade reading list read and reported on—even that damn Paddington bear, torturously dull but the last thing on the list—and all of his Scholastic points accumulated, with no beetle shells or toothpicks or cardboard boxes or broken bats handy, with Dan Shock still engaged in the turkey-head argument with Miss Sunday—an argument that would surely last until lunchtime—Sean Carswell felt he had no choice but to stand from his chair, walk across the room, and punch Dan Shock in the mouth.

Much to her embarrassment on this day, Sean Carswell's mother was a teacher at this backwater, swampland elementary school. All were called before the principal: Miss

Sunday, Mrs. Shock, Mrs. Carswell, Sean Carswell, and Dan Shock with his brand new fat lip. Miss Sunday gloated. She and Mrs. Carswell did not get along. Perhaps, Miss Sunday felt a sense of vindication. Mrs. Carswell's other two, her eldest son and young daughter, were poster children for the school. The male one an exceptional athlete, the female so cute she was a heartbreak waiting to happen. Both were appropriately unmotivated students. Not like young Sean Carswell. Who did he think he was with all his books and his memorized multiplication tables and his obsessive talk of ukuleles? For Miss Sunday, Sean Carswell's misbehavior was his mother's comeuppance. Glee emanated from the edges of her words as she described the assault on poor little Dan Shock and his pinkie-headed turkey.

Dan Shock sat in his little chair with his fat lip jutted out in a mixture of pain and humiliation. Mrs. Shock was, well, just shocked by it all. Mrs. Carswell expressed an adequate sense of remorse. Only Sean Carswell refused to play his role. He sat cross-armed and snarling. If this slow parade of stupidity continued, he'd sock 'em all in the mouth.

This wouldn't do for Principal Cowling. Suspension, particularly of a teacher's son, was not a scenario under consideration at this point. He proposed, and it was agreed upon by five of the six parties present, that Sean Carswell should spend his class time taking notes instead of reading library books and punching his classmates.

So note-taking was piled upon the indignity of a rural Florida public school education.

Sean Carswell's mother gave him a spiral notebook that a fourth grader failed to rescue from lost and found in a timely manner. Sean Carswell began taking notes. He documented all of the activities of the classroom. In the evening, he sat at the kitchen counter while his mother prepared a meal of whatever innards were on sale at Harry's Meat Market. Let's say on this one particular Wednesday night, dinner was pan-fried chicken livers with macaroni and cheese and canned green beans. Sean Carswell's brother and sister sat in front of the television, arguing over whether they'd watch *Eight Is Enough* or *The Life of Grizzly Adams* when primetime finally rolled around. This argument could last for hours, so Sean Carswell's brother and sister began it hours before the actual programming began. His father watched the evening news, somehow unperturbed by the failing picture tube that cast the world according to Walter Cronkite into an alien green pallor.

Sean Carswell read the day's notes: *We are reading about the Jamestown settlement. Caryn Paige thinks it is the "jam is town set, set, set, emmm." Paul Fulmer falls deeper in love with every word Caryn can't read. I hope someone else will get to read the next paragraph. I may be old enough to drive before Caryn gets through the word "Pocahontas."*

"How long did she let Caryn read?" Mrs. Carswell asked.

"Three or four hours," Sean Carswell said.

"No," Mrs. Carswell said. "You're not going to get me on that one."

"It's true. I read all the way up to the Civil War before

she stopped pronouncing the 'h' in John Smith."

Mrs. Carswell smiled and looked at her husband. He was the one who had given the kid this sense of humor.

Sean Carswell skipped ahead to the math notes: *Dave Gast has to figure out what 3 x 5 equals. The sum was 15 when Miss Sunday asked him yesterday. Could it be the same today? Is it possible for his brain to hold the equation 3 x 5 = 15 for twenty-four hours? The answer is no. Will he guess every number he can think of until he hits fifteen? Yes. His guesses so far: 35, 2, 17, 99, 26, 57, and 83. I know why Miss Sunday is so interested in the number 15. It's because...*

Sean Carswell stopped before reading the mean statement that followed.

Mrs. Carswell turned the chicken livers in the pan. Sean Carswell's brother and sister's argument devolved into name calling. Walter Cronkite and Mr. Carswell worried about inflation together. Outside the Carswell household, the popular kids in Sean Carswell's second grade class plotted new ways to sabotage their education.

The next day, Miss Sunday insisted upon seeing Sean Carswell's class notes. She forgave everything until she arrived at the line, "*I know why Miss Sunday is so interested in the number 15. It's because each of Miss Sunday's butt cheeks are 3 x 5 inches wide.*" Another rendezvous was scheduled with Principal Cowling.

This session's compromise was much more agreeable to Sean Carswell. To Miss Sunday's chagrin, Principal Cowling suggested that Sean Carswell should be allowed to build ukuleles in the back corner of the classroom once all of his day's work was finished. This may have been the defining moment for the future carpenter-turned-author.

He convinced his mother that he needed a knife to shape the neck. His mother dug up an old, rusted number she'd found in a garage drawer when she moved into her house. She rubbed the blade against the concrete floor until it was dull enough to be bullied by a butter knife. Sean Carswell took the dull knife back to the garage and massaged it against his father's sharpening stone until it was equally as sharp as the pocket knives half of the boys in school wore in their back pockets. He carried the knife and an old two-by-four to school the next day.

Take a moment now to picture Sean Carswell in the back corner of his elementary school classroom, sitting at a tiny workbench that his janitor buddy, Earl, constructed for him out of a one-legged card table. A column of obsolete textbooks bound together with duct tape replaces one of the missing legs; the gym teacher's abandoned disciplinary paddle replaces another. The final corner is propped up by the cubbies where students store their lunches and, on the one cold morning of the year, their windbreakers. The seven-year-old Sean Carswell may look, in your mind's eye, like the current version of the man. His gray hair would glisten under the school's fluorescent lights. His classmates would be dazzled by his sweet goatee. His seven-year-old hands would be covered in scars and cracks like the alligator-skin purse a swampland hunter makes for his second-favorite girlfriend. We'll have to revise this, somewhat. Turn some of that gray (though not all; our best intelligence dates the graying of Sean Carswell's hair to his kindergarten year) into a blond bowl cut. Shave the goatee and imagine against all better judgment a chin. Shrink him to kid size. Create your own montage of him whittling down the two-by-four into the neck of a soprano ukulele while Dave Gast slaughters mathematics and Caryn Paige builds speed bumps between every written word. This montage should include Sean Carswell running the neck through a pencil box, then gluing the pencil box together to serve as the uke body. The next shot will show Johnny Wilkinson breaking all of his classmates' pencils when he's bored with the diamonds Dan Shock cuts out of construction paper while imagining Valentine hearts. Sean Carswell will respond by breaking Johnny Wilkinson's long pencil in half, sharpening both ends, and turning it into a ukulele bridge. An additional scene will include Miss Sunday becoming Mrs. Matthews and spending an entire school day with a slide show of wedding pictures and stories of a honeymoon spent at the Bithlo stock car races. The last shots chronicle the completion of the ukulele: finish nails absconded from neighborhood construction sites being glued down for frets; eye bolts shoplifted from Ace Hardware being transformed into functional tuners; and, finally, fishing lines being strung on the masterpiece.

Everything changed at recess once the ukulele was built. Sean Carswell took to entertaining the rabble with original songs about the issues of the day: six's fear of seven, footprints in the butter, Dwayne the Bathtub (who's dwowning), and the cross between an elephant and a rhinoceros. Mrs. Matthews was far from ecstatic about the evolution of Sean Carswell's ukulele, but she was happy with the crowd at recess. Some students sat cross-legged in a semicircle around Sean Carswell. Other students twisted and hopped and shook and spun around in movements that seven-year-olds like to call "dancing." Sean Carswell leaned against the monkey bars, strumming and singing. No one seemed to need monitoring, which freed up Mrs. Matthews to smoke with her fellow second grade teacher, Miss Shore, and fantasize about the day when Miss Shore, too, would become a Mrs. Something Else.

Only, on this Thursday, long before Sean Carswell's brother and sister would start their fight over whether to watch *What's Happening!!* or *CHiPs*, Sean Carswell started singing the classroom favorite: "Mother May I? (Spell Cup)." A lull came over the conversation between Mrs. Matthews and Miss Shore. The last refrains of the song were belted out in a call-and-response style. Sean Carswell sang, "Mother May I?" His classmates sang out, "C-U-P."

Miss Shore asked, "What's that kid singing?"

Mrs. Matthews listened.

Sean Carswell improvised the ending a bit. This was a schoolyard favorite. Instead of "mother," he called out the names of his classmates, singing, "Todd Hoagland may I?" while the class sang, "C-U-P."

"Mark Bishop may I?"

"C-U-P."

"Wendy Sturman may I?"

"C-U-P."

"Mary Lynn Honeycutt may I?"

"C-U-P."

Miss Shore giggled. Mrs. Matthews contemplated putting an end to the song. But she'd just started a cigarette.

Sean Carswell ran through all the names of his classmates except Rodney Butler's. That name elicited hesitation. Rodney was the only genuinely slow kid in the class. He was always a risk during this song because, one recess period not too long earlier, Judy Flynn asked to see him pee and he obliged. Both were sent to the principal. Neither returned to school for two weeks. With no other names and the refrain coming around so quickly, Sean Carswell acted without full deliberation. He sang, "Rodney Butler may I?"

With Judy Flynn looking straight at Rodney Butler and singing perhaps the loudest, the class belted out, "C-U-P."

In the wave of excitement, Rodney dropped his shorts to his ankles, lifted his T-shirt over his prodigious belly, and watered the black schoolyard dirt. The class roared. Sean Carswell accompanied their laughter with a few more measures on his homemade ukulele. Miss Shore leaned into Mrs. Matthews' shoulder and snickered. "Look at Rodney's little dickey-doo."

The slightest laugh was rerouted from Mrs. Matthews' pursed lips but managed to escape through her nostrils. She looked at her half-smoked cigarette and decided that intervention was still not yet necessary. Rodney had finished and shaken and hiked up his shorts once again. Sean Carswell strummed without singing.

What Mrs. Matthews couldn't know was that, with no more names left to sing, with Rodney's spectacle outshining his song, Sean Carswell had to take his art to the next level. When the hoi polloi settled, he sang out the last possible line of the refrain: "Mrs. Matthews may I?"

Instead of the usual "C-U-P," Sean Carswell's classmates responded with silence. In his mind's ear, Sean Carswell heard the "C" and the "U," but before the "P" could slide into the song, Mrs. Matthews wrapped her nicotine-stained fingers around his upper arm and started dragging him principal-ward, with ukulele in tow.

On this final infraction, Mr. Carswell was called into the meeting of Mrs. Matthews and Principal Cowling. Suspension at this point had moved beyond consideration and into implementation. Mrs. Carswell would have to withstand the gossip and barbs of breakroom politics for the rest of the school year. Sean Carswell would spend one day of his institutionally mandated two-week break in his father's truck, completing the schoolwork he was missing. He would spend the other weekdays working a series of small jobs on his father's construction site.

At the end of the suspension, Sean Carswell's ukulele would be returned to him. His father would drive him home from the day's job site. Mr. Carswell would tousle his son's slightly graying blond bowl cut and say, "Don't worry, kid. I always find a way to fuck things up, too."

Sean Carswell would pluck at the strings of his pencil box ukulele, seeking a way to turn that sentiment into a song.

Acknowledgements

Thanks to Pam Houston and Patricia Geary for reading the stories in which I made them each a main character, and for giving me their blessings to publish those stories. They both have also done me the huge favor of writing blurbs for my books. That means the world to me. I borrowed passages, true stories, and stylistic tricks from all the authors in this collection. Thanks to each of them for being a muse and an inspiration. Thanks in advance to the living authors in this collection and the estates of the dead authors for recognizing the difference between homage and plagiarism.

Jim Ruland and Mickey Hess have been reading my manuscripts and giving me feedback for years now. Thanks to both of them for the help on this book. Brad Monsma, Mary Adler, Bob Mayberry, and Sofia Samatar workshopped several of these stories with me in our writing group. Without their encouragement, I might not have tried to publish any of this. Ben Loory blew my mind when the two of us did a reading in San Diego, and he had an Elmore Leonard story that seemed to fit in the spirit of this collection that I had just finished. Thanks to him for endorsing this book. Several editors published these stories before they became a collection. Thanks to all of them. Robert Lasner and Elizabeth Clementson took a chance on this book. I can't thank them enough for that.

Most importantly, thanks to Felizon Vidad. It takes a very special person to be married to a guy who spends a lot of his time obsessing on ukuleles and other things literary.